THE GOSPELS OF
TSAR IVAN ALEXANDER

ЄВAГГЄЛIЄ СТО ω Iω AН НА ⁘ А̃

Ъ НАЧАЛѢ БѢ ШЄ СЛОВО · И СЛОВО БѢ
ω БA · И БЪ БѢ СЛОВО · СЄ БѢ ИСКОНИ
ω БA · ВЬСѢ ТѢ МЬ БЫША · И БЄЗ НЄ
ГО НИ ЧТО ЖЄ БЫ · ЄЖЄ БЫ · ВЪ ТОМЬ
ЖИВОТЪ БѢ · И ЖИВОБѢ СВѢТ
Ч̃ЛКОМЪ · И СВѢТ ВЪ ТЬ МѢ СВѢ
ТИТЪ · И ТЬ МА ЄГО НЄ ωБЪӔТ ·

THE GOSPELS OF
TSAR IVAN ALEXANDER

Ekaterina Dimitrova

THE BRITISH LIBRARY

Acknowledgements
The British Library would like to thank the following for their generous contributions towards the production of this book:

The Open Society, Sofia, Bulgaria ✆
The employees of Cadbury Beverages working in the Central and East European Division.

Dedication
In memory of my ancestors, Dukus and Engilis of Djerman

Study of the Gospels manuscript inspired me to believe that no monograph should exceed the size of the work which has been central to western civilization for so long, the story of the Life of Christ. Fortunately I have been saved from any danger, the credit for which goes to Janet Backhouse who established the pattern and format for The British Library's series devoted to its outstanding illuminated manuscripts, of which this is the sixth volume. I am indebted to Sava Peic, who was the first to encourage me to study the manuscript and who has spared no efforts in subsequent discussions and in assisting me in finding obscure references. I am greatly obliged to Scot McKendrick who has taken a deep interest in my study and has dedicated valuable help and expertise to the work. To Anne Young, who undertook the painstaking job of correcting and editing a foreigner's writing, I am particularly grateful. I owe special thanks to Bruce Barker-Benfield for his kind assistance when I studied the Bodleian Library's valuable sources. My thanks are also due to the photographer Laurence Pordes for the perfect job he has done, and to Tchavdar Yanev for contributing the diagrammatic drawings.

I am indebted to Dr Mary McRobert and Dr W. Ryan for their helpful suggestions related to the study of the 'magic square'. I am also grateful to The British Library staff who have facilitated my research; to the Vatican Library, Rome, for permission to reproduce an illustration from a manuscript in its collections; and to the London Mathematical Society for their attempts to resolve the mystery of the manuscript's 'magic square' with the aid of computers. I am also grateful to Hazel Marsden for her help in studying the obscure French text of Dionysius' *Hermeneia*, to Gina Douglas for providing me with valuable materials, and to John Marsden for his constant technical assistance.

I am greatly obliged to the Open Society, Sofia, and to Cadbury Beverages Eastern European division who have taken such an interest in the project and have generously sponsored its publication. I am particularly grateful to His Eminence Simeon, Metropolitan of the Western European Bulgarian Patriarchate, to John Stancioff, the former Bulgarian Ambassador to Great Britain, and to Boris Christov, for their personal interest in and encouragement of my research. Finally, I am grateful to my family for their vital support of the entire work; I remain humble before the exciting opportunity to undertake it.

Ekaterina Dimitrova, June 1994

(*Front cover*) Tsar Ivan Alexander, from the royal portrait, the masterpiece of the Gospels (f.3, detail, enlarged).

(*Back cover*) Christ and the apostles after the Resurrection (f.272v, detail).

(*Half-title page*) The 'magic square' with the inscription 'Iw Alexander Tsarya Tetravaggel' ('the Four Gospels of Tsar Ivan Alexander') (f.273).

(*Frontispiece*) Headpiece of the Gospel of St John (f.213).

(*Title-page*) John the Evangelist presenting his Gospel to Tsar Ivan Alexander (f.272v).

First published 1994 by
The British Library, Great Russell Street, London WC1B 3DG

British Library Cataloguing in Publication Data
A cataloguing record for this book is available from The British Library.

ISBN 0-7123-0349-9

Photography by Laurence Pordes
Designed by James Shurmer
Typeset in Linotron Bembo by Bexhill Phototypesetters, Bexhill on Sea, East Sussex
Printed in Singapore by Craft Print

CONTENTS

ІАКѠВЖ РѺДНЮДѪ ИБРАТНѪ ЕГО.

ЇѠДАЖЕРѺДНФАРЕСАНЗАРѠ

ФА AMAPЫ · ФАРЕСЪ ЖЕ РѺДН ҆ НЄСРО
ЛА · ЕСРОЛЖЕ РѺДН АРАМА · АРА
МЪ ЖЕ РѺДН АМИННАДАВА · АМИННА
ДАВЖЕ РѺДН ҆ НААССОНА · НААССѠ
НЖЕ РѺДН ҆ САЛМѠНА · САЛМѠН
ЖЕ РѺДН ВОѠZАѠРАХАВЫ · ВО
ѠZЖЕ РѺДН ҆ ѠВНДА, ѠРОУѲЫ.
ѠВНДЖЕ, РѺДН ҆ ЇЕССЕА · ЇЕССЕН
ЖЕ РѺДН, ДАВЫДАЦР҃Ѣ :

INTRODUCTION

The *Oxford Dictionary of Byzantium* (1991) makes no mention of the Gospels of Tsar Ivan Alexander in its entry for 'frieze-gospels', and very few students from the Slavonic department of the University of London are aware that this superb Cyrillic manuscript is nearby on permanent exhibition in The British Library galleries. And yet the Gospels, created in Bulgaria in the mid-fourteenth century, is the masterpiece of a culture in which the importance of the Cyrillic alphabet is, uniquely, celebrated with an annual feast day of letters on 24 May. Moreover, it contains an outstanding portrait of Tsar Ivan Alexander and his family which remains today a powerful symbol of Bulgarian nationhood – the crowning achievement of the last Bulgarian cultural and political Renaissance before the country fell under the yoke of the Ottoman Turks in 1393.

The Gospels of Tsar Ivan Alexander (now British Library, Additional MS 39627) is a monument of the last revival of literature and the arts in medieval Bulgaria, 500 years after the christianization of the country and the introduction of the Cyrillic script. The Gospels was commissioned by the Tsar for his library in 1355 and was completed in just one year. Its 367 miniatures are a powerful testimony to the rich artistic achievement of the Turnovo school of manuscript illumination, combining archaic and ecclesiastical styles with discernible Renaissance elements. The Gospels' masterpiece – the portrait of the Tsar himself and his family – is an outstanding example of medieval Orthodox art, and indeed the whole manuscript had a seminal influence upon later Orthodox works. The manuscript was written by a single scribe, Simeon, who recorded his achievement in an unusual colophon. A number of hands can be detected in the miniatures, though the artists remain conventionally anonymous. In addition to the miniatures, the manuscript contains a fascinating palindrome, a geometric word puzzle in which the title 'the Four Gospels of Tsar Ivan Alexander' can be read both backwards and forwards countless times. Together with the use of geometry of sacred significance in some of the miniatures, discussed in this book for the first time, this 'magic square' offers a fascinating insight into the nature of medieval orthodox spirituality.

The Gospels survived the fall of Turnovo under the Ottoman invasion of 1393, probably transported to safety across the Danube to Moldavia. Little is known of its subsequent history until the early seventeenth century when it was housed in the monastery of St Paul on Mount Athos in Greece. It was here that the 23-year-old Hon. Robert Curzon, in highly fortuitous circumstances, contrived to acquire the manuscript, having recognised it as 'one of the most curious monuments of bygone days to be found in any library in Europe'. It was ultimately bequeathed to the British Museum in 1917 and passed into the collections of The British Library on its foundation in 1973.

(Opposite page) 1 The genealogy of Christ; Jacob and his sons (f.6v).

Bulgaria
borders 1355

0   50 miles 100
0   50   100 kms

SERBIA

Belgrade

Bdin

RIVER   DANUBE

DOBRUDJA

BLACK SEA

RYANTRA

Pliska

Turnovo

Preslav

Varna

KOSOVO

Sofia

BALKAN MOUNTAINS

Velbujd

RILA

Phillipopolis

PRILEP

MACEDONIA

VELBUJD

BYZANTIUM

Constantinople

Prilep

Ochrid

Mt Athos

AEGEAN SEA

(*Above*)
2 Medieval Bulgaria, *c.*1355.

(*Right*)
3 Artist's impression of Turnovo during the late Second Bulgarian Empire, mid-fourteenth century (artist Ts Lavrenov).

THE HISTORICAL BACKGROUND

The early Bulgarian and Byzantine Empires

Just as the great in Holiness Tsar Constantine and his mother Helena unearthed the life-giving cross of our Lord, so is the creation of this manuscript of the four gospels.

Colophon, the Gospels of Tsar Ivan Alexander, f.275

The Gospels of Tsar Ivan Alexander is the outstanding treasure of an artistic and spiritual Renaissance which came to fruition in Bulgaria in the mid-fourteenth century. Its creation marks one of the supreme achievements of Bulgarian and Byzantine culture, but also its final flourishing, shortly before the collapse of the Balkans under the invasion of the Ottoman Turks. When Simeon, the scribe of the Gospels, compared the achievement of Tsar Ivan Alexander in commissioning the manuscript with that of Constantine the Great, he could not have anticipated that these two events would come to symbolize both the rise of Christian civilization and the beginning of its greatest testing.

According to legend, the rise of Byzantium as a world power began with the divine omen of the discovery of the Holy Cross by Constantine the Great (312–337AD). Its history is certainly inseparable from that of the Orthodox church; for, although only baptised on his death-bed, Constantine inspired an empire which effectively transformed the imperial civil organisation of ancient Rome into a Christian order. He divided his Empire into two parts, with capitals in Rome in the west and Constantinople in the east, and consolidated its spiritual power base through the clarification of Orthodox doctrine and rigorous attacks on the various sects and heresies which threatened to undermine it. The reign of Justinian (527–610) further ensured the Empire's stability by constituting its civil law in the Codex Justinianus.

Meanwhile, the fourth and fifth centuries had seen a great migration of nomadic and warlike peoples from Asia which changed the face of Europe. The Bulgars formed 'Great Bulgaria' between the Black and Caspian Seas and it was during the reign of Khan Kubrat ('the lord of the Huns', 581–641AD) that friendly relations were first established, in 619, with the Byzantine Emperor Heraclius (reigned 610–641). Some Bulgars settled in the Volga area, others in Panonia, Lombardia and Macedonia, while those led by Khan Asparuch (reigned 681–701) conquered the area south of the Danube in the Balkans. In 681, after a decisive victory at the mouth of the Danube over the army of Constantine IV (reigned 668–685), modern Bulgaria was founded, with its capital at Pliska.

The Byzantine Empire's struggle with the Persians and Arabs for supremacy in Eastern Europe and the Eastern Mediterranean during the seventh and eighth centuries was significantly aided by the Bulgarian Khan Tervel (reigned 701–718) who assisted in the restoration of Justinian II in 705 and in the repulsion of the Arabs in 717–718. However, this success was followed by the spiritual upheaval created by the iconoclastic movement, combined with a long and exhausting conflict between the Empire and the Bulgars who now demanded the same imperial status for their own state. The Bulgars' insurrection culminated in 813 with the siege of Constantinople by Khan Krum (803–814) who sought to expand the country as a third European power alongside Charlemagne's Empire in the west and Byzantium.

The triumph of the Orthodox doctrine over iconoclasm in 843 marked the beginning of a new phase of expansion for the Orthodox creed. The creation of the Glagolitic and Cyrillic scripts (c.855, c.885) and the christianization of the Bulgars in 865 culminated in a golden age of learning and the arts under the patronage of Tsar Simeon (reigned 893–927).

Political Decline and the Ottoman Invasion

After a period of stability during the tenth and eleventh centuries under the warrior-emperors of the Macedonian dynasty, Byzantium began its final political decline, marked by the loss of Anatolia to the Seljuk Turks after the battle of Mantzikert in 1071. Constantinople fell to the crusaders in 1204 and although it was

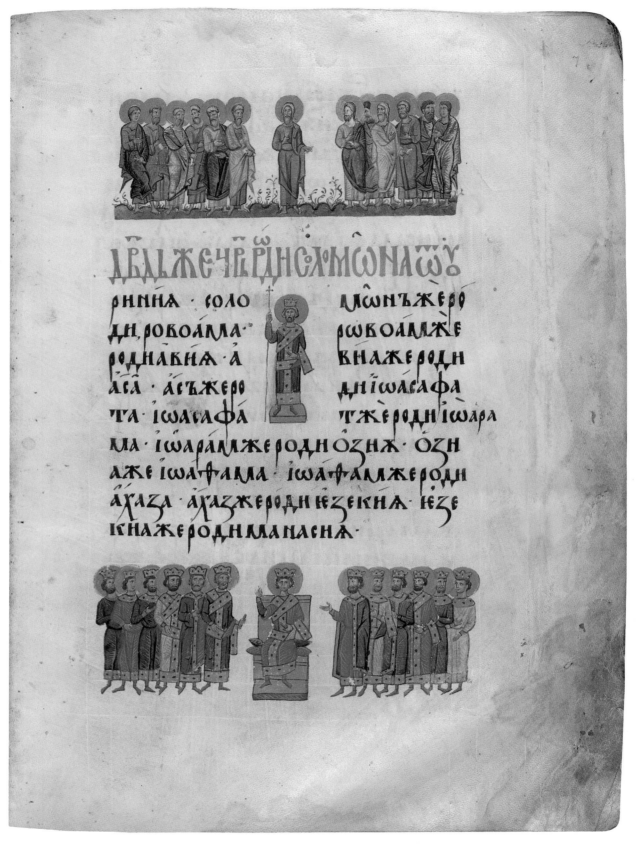

4 The genealogy of Christ; Juda and his brothers, Kings David and Solomon, at his court (f.7).

Ꙇⰵⰾⰻⰻⱅⰵ ꙗⰽⱁ ⱂⱃⰻⰴⱁⱈⱏ ⰲⱏ ⰲⱃⱑ
ⱋⰻⰾⰻⱃⰰ ⱂⰰ ⰸⰵⰿⰾⱑ · ⱀⰵ ⱂⱃⰻⰻⰴⱁ
ⱈⱏ ⰲⱏ ⰲⱃⱑⱋⰻⰾⰻⱃⰰ , ⱀⱏ ⰿⰵⱍⱏ ·
ⱂⱃⰻⰻⰴⱁⱈⱏ ⰱⱁ ⱃⰰⰸⰾⱘⱍⰻⱅⰻ ⱍⰾⰽⰰ ,
ⱀⰰ ⱁⱌⰰ ⱄⰲⱁⰵⰳⱁ · ⰻ ⰴⱏⱋⰵⱃⱏ ⱀⰰ
ⰿⱅⱃⱐ ⱄⰲⱁⰶ · ⰻ ⱀⰵⰲⱑⱄⱅⱘ ⱀⰰ ⰲⰵ

5 Christ teaching spiritual majesty (f.32v).

recovered in 1261 the subsequent advance of the Turks proved beyond control. In 1387 the Serbs were defeated at Kosovo, and five years later Belgrade, the Serbian capital, fell. On 17 July 1393 the Turks took Turnovo, the cultural and political capital of Bulgaria. The final blow came on 26 May 1453, with the fall of Constantinople and the death of its last emperor, Constantine IX, killed fighting on the ramparts of the city during the last days of the siege. Twelve centuries of Byzantine glory and splendour had ended.

The dynastic feuding of the Balkan states had in part contributed to the growth of the Ottoman Empire. They certainly failed to unite against the common threat of the advancing Turks and had even invited them to participate as mercenaries in Byzantium's troubled domestic, political, and civil affairs. When, after several bloody contests for the throne, Michael VIII became emperor, the Palaeologan dynasty which had ruled the Empire for two centuries since 1259, was in decline. The aristocracy, finding themselves free from the imperial authority of Constantinople, demanded autonomous status, effectively reinventing the Hellenic concept of city states, secured with armies and mercenaries. The devastating civil war which broke out in 1341 finally eroded the strength of an Empire which had once been regarded with awe by the west as a seat of civilization and learning.

The Hesychast Ideology

The ecclesiastical nature of the Empire ensured that, from its foundation, spiritual affairs were central to its conduct in the Balkans. In the early fourteenth century the Orthodox faith too was put to the test by the new spiritual movement of Hesychasm, introduced from the east. By requiring a form of inactive self-discipline, in isolated, uninterrupted prayer, the Hesychast ideology diverted concentration and energy away from social activity to 'Hesychia' – silent contemplation – claiming that this was the only condition in which God's light would be perceived and in which all contradictions would be mysteriously resolved. Brought to Mount Athos by Gregory of Sinai, and further spread by Gregory Palamas, this highly spiritual, but socially unproductive doctrine penetrated the whole Balkan Orthodox world, causing irreparable ethical controversies both within the Balkan community and in its relation to the rest of the Catholic world. The man of action was replaced by the man of thought, and it seems

that the Balkan peoples were more receptive to the idea of cultural retreat rather than preparation for war.

In 1341 the Hesychast doctrine was passionately defended against the Catholic church's embassy of Barlaam, and in 1351 the Ecumenical Council in Constantinople established 'the uncreated light of Mount Tabor' as an article of Greek Orthodox faith. Turnovo Council, with the approval of Tsar Ivan Alexander, simultaneously incorporated it into the Bulgarian Orthodox ideal. The doctrine was later to be viewed by the monks of Mount Athos as the apple of discord which had divided the Orthodox church into 'latinophiles' and 'latinophobes'. As the Hon. Robert Curzon perceptively remarked:

What a difference it would have made to the affairs of Europe if the embassy of Barlaam had succeeded! The Turks would not have been now in possession of Constantinople; and in many points of difference having been mutually conceded by the two great divisions of the church, perhaps the Reformation never would have taken place.

Robert Curzon, *Visits to Monasteries of the Levant* (London, 1916, p.414)

From Iconoclasm to the Palaeologan Renaissance

Against this background of political and spiritual turmoil and the tightening of the Ottoman ring around the Balkans rose the Palaeologan Renaissance, a golden age of cultural achievement in the late Byzantine Empire. The Palaeologan dynasty (1259–1453) set out to exceed the splendour of the preceding Comnenian dynasty (1081–1261), and patronage of the arts was one of its highest priorities. This Renaissance was the final phase of the post-iconoclastic revival in art.

Iconoclasm had risen to prominence in 726 when the Emperor Leo II publicly supported the position of several bishops in Asia Minor who condemned the veneration of images. The doctrine denied the holiness of icons and rejected their veneration, decreeing that every form of pictorial representation, whether on panels, walls, holy vessels, altar cloths or any other vehicle for artistic depiction in Christian churches, should be destroyed. This denial of religious imagery struck at the heart of the Byzantine Empire, for which the iconography of the life of Christ provided a significant spiritual resource. The ideology flourished for two periods during the eighth and ninth centuries (726–778

ЕЖЕНСП ⲀЬ НВⲀⳍⲀСТⲀ · КЬⳀ КРⲀТНСⲀⳠⲰ IО
РⲀⲀⲚⲐ · НВЕⲆⲐ ШЕСⲀ Ⲁ Ⲁ Ⲭ ОⲘ Ⳓ КЬНⲠОⲨСТЫ
Ⲛ Ⲁ. Ⲓ Ⲓ. Ⲃ Ⲅ. ... ⲘⲐ ...... С ... ... Ⲁ Ⲓ Ⲁ Ⲕ О Ⲓ О ⲘⲒ

6 The genealogy of Christ; the descent of Joseph into Paradise (above), and Joseph teaching (below) (f.147).

and 814–842). It is now difficult to determine how much early Christian art perished under its influence.

The end of iconoclasm, on 11 March 843, resulted in a revised theory of the icon as a symbol, making a clear distinction between worship, which was rendered only to God, and veneration, which honoured the icon itself. This doctrine, first propagated by John of Damascus (652–730), became the touchstone for successive artistic movements in the Balkans from the ninth to the fourteenth centuries, interrupted only by the invasion of the crusaders of the fourth Crusade (1204–1261).

The Palaeologan Renaissance was the final manifestation of this movement, which explored the idea of the icon in two major and distinctive ways. An elegant linearism replaced the monumentality of the Comnenian style, and marked a movement towards representational rather than symbolic forms, while a new artistic interest in human aspects of religious subjects emerged. The church of Chora Monastery in Constantinople (Istanbul) is an outstanding example of these qualities in Palaeologan art. In addition, the interpretation of the canon in a more vivid and expressive style infused with local colour was particularly characteristic of Balkan iconography and paralleled the contemporary humanist movement of the Italian Renaissance.

By the late fourteenth century, patronage of the arts in Byzantium was conducted on a smaller scale, by feudal families and benefactors, while in the Balkans the king remained the principal patron. In Bulgaria, in a forerunner to the Turnovo revival, the frescoes of Boyana church near Sofia were commissioned by the Assen dynasty in 1259; they survive as testimony to the best representational qualities of works of art of the period. The Ivanovo rock church, built a hundred years later, testifies to the inventive exploration of the interaction between nature and art. It was at this time that Tsar Ivan Alexander established a cultural capital at Turnovo, encouraging the development of a homogenous artistic style, language reform and the most active centre of book production in the Balkans, of which his Gospels was the crowning achievement.

TSAR IVAN ALEXANDER AND THE CREATION OF THE GOSPELS

Very little is known about the background to the creation of the Gospels of Tsar Ivan Alexander, though as the scribe's colophon notes it was clearly an event of extraordinary spiritual significance. The production of the Gospels enjoyed the Tsar's special patronage and it was the most important of many similar undertakings achieved during his reign. The work was commissioned in 1355, probably from the principal scriptorium in Turnovo, and was completed in the astonishingly short period of one year. Turnovo, built on the hills of Tsarevez and Trapezitsa overlooking the river Yantra, had been established as the seat of the Assen dynasty, to which Ivan Alexander belonged, with the restoration of the Bulgarian empire, following the Byzantine domination of 1018–1185. The city continued the tradition of artistic splendour of Pliska and Preslav, the previous Bulgarian capitals, and was famous for its churches, libraries and palaces (*see* p.8).

The Gospels, designed as a private treasure for the monarch, contains many personal references, including the fascinating palindrome of ownership, which is unique (*see* pages 26–27 and half-title page). Other manuscripts from the period make reference to the Tsar's religious devotion, his patronage of the Turnovo school of arts, his greatness as a ruler, and his erudition. From the colophon of a fourteenth-century Turnovo copy of the Acts of the Apostles we learn of his high scholarly standards, as he:

embellished with all virtues, wanted, along with all other good acts, a translation of this book from Greek into Bulgarian, to be undertaken with complete endeavour and spiritual love.

Published by Dinekov, P., *Hristomatya po Starobulgarska Literatura*, 1967, Sofia, p.322

Ivan Alexander's encouragement ensured a favourable environment for writers, artists, and the enlightened clergy to initiate a revival of interest in classical literature, indigenous art and theosophy. He took a deep interest in the theology of Hesychasm, promoting its anthropocentric ideal within the traditional Orthodox school at the Turnovo Councils of 1351 and 1359 and banning the various sects. Simeon, the scribe of the Gospels, describes the practical manifestation of this philosophy in the creation of the manuscript, writing in the colophon:

. . . The vision and the acts of Christ are like a spring which appears on dry land; he who is thirsty and drinks from it shall never be thirsty again; he will enjoy in his soul, rejoice in his heart and in his mind, and this will become his innermost treasure, the fulfilment of his heart-kingdom. This revival, inspired by the faithful, noble, Christ-loving, and God's elected autocrat Ivan Alexander, is like a candelabrum, left by the old kings and forgotten in darkness. The Christ-loving Tsar Ivan Alexander revived it as a divine inspiration, in the composing of a copy from the Greek into our own Slavonic language; the copy was bound and covered with a silver-gilt wooden board, while the inside was illuminated with the life-giving images of the Lord and His glorious disciple Jesus.

The Gospels of Tsar Ivan Alexander, ff.274–274v

There were two major aspects of this humanist revival: a complete recreation of the New Testament in images and text, translated into the Bulgarian language, as exemplified by Ivan Alexander's Gospels, and a fresh interest in the historical context of the Tsar's reign. The intensive book production carried out at Turnovo during the period thus included chronicles, biographies and historical tracts, evidence of enlightened learning and creativity, as well as gospels, psalters and liturgical books. Many of the surviving volumes bear witness, either directly or indirectly to the Tsar's achievements. The Turnovo version of the World Chronicle of Constantine Manasses, commissioned by the Tsar in 1345, and now in the Vatican Library (Vatican, MS Slav. 2), is a rare example of a bringing together of Orthodox ideas, historical detail and classical mythology, retelling, amongst others, the story of the Trojan war for the fourteenth-century Bulgarian reader. The Tomic Psalter, commissioned in 1360 and now in Moscow Public Library (Moscow, CIM, MS Syn. 2752), is the cornerstone of an important innovation in Byzantine art, the

(*Opposite*) 7 (*above*), 8 (*below*) Battle scenes illustrating the prophesy of the destruction of Jerusalem (above, f.200, below, f.123).

ꙗ҆ко приближи́сѧ за́поуст҄ѣ́нїе є҆му҄

То́гдаⷭ҇ сꙋ́щїй вⸯ і҆ꙋде́н, да бѣ́гаютъ въ

капⷧа́тъ · и҆ ꙁиꙁбра́нныхⸯ ра́дⸯ на҆же́н
ꙁбⸯра прѣ́кратидⷩ҇ни · н҄

Н то́гда а҆ще́ кⷮо ре́тъ сⷭе сⷣⷯе сⷭе ѿⷦвⷣⷣе, не и҆ма́

illumination of the principal Akathistos Hymn in honour of the mother of God (Theotokos), exemplifying both the artistic creativity of the Turnovo school and the influence of the liturgy on art. A panegyric from a psalter now in the library of the Bulgarian Academy of Sciences praises the Tsar as 'a second Alexander of Antiquity' for his 'military might', while an act relating to the Zographos Monastery on Mount Athos offers important evidence of Ivan Alexander's diverse religious patronage:

This gold-written act of my kingdom is issued to order the above mentioned monastery of my kingdom to possess and have use of the village of Hantakh, indisputably, with all its properties and incomes; further – that this honoured monastery should not be troubled to pay the former amount of 50 perpers, which was the tax for wheat, surplus and masonry, because this has been obtained from his highness the Greek prince Calojan Palaeologus, the beloved nephew and kinsman of my kingdom.

The Tsar's political activities were less rewarding. The dynastic marriages which he entered into did not guarantee political stability within the Balkans as he had hoped. His first wife, Theodora, was a Wallachian princess, while his sister, Helena, married the Serbian King Stefan Dušan. His daughter Maria was betrothed to the Byzantine Prince Andronicus Palaeologus, while his other son-in-law was the Serbian Prince Constantine. None of these marriages provided the political unity required against the Ottoman Turks. Ivan Alexander's second marriage to the Jewish-born Sara, who converted to Christianity as Theodora in 1345, created a battle for the succession. The traditionally rigid rule regarding Bulgarian heredity was altered and Ivan Stracimir, the Tsar's first son from his first marriage and legitimate heir to the throne, was disinherited. This decision was later to cause a devastating division of Bulgaria into three autonomous parts. Ivan Shishman, the first son from the Tsar's second marriage, was proclaimed Tsar upon the death of his father in 1371 and was crowned at Turnovo, while Ivan Stracimir retreated bitterly to Bdin. The Dobrudja region was left to be ruled by the wealthy feudal family, the Dobrotica. The isolated Ivan Shishman tried to cope with the advancing Ottoman Turks by entering into treaties with them, all of which finally collapsed in 1393 when Turnovo, lacking any efficient military defence, was attacked and burnt to the ground.

Tsar Ivan Alexander died on 17 February 1371, along with his dream of making Turnovo a new Constantinople, another Rome, a cultural centre for Orthodox civilization. None the less, the very small part of his library which has come down to us is remarkable for its embodiment of the values of his reign, exemplified at its best in the creation of his Gospels.

The Tsar and his family are prominently portrayed in the Gospels' masterpiece which appears at the front of the volume (fig.11). The portrait represents the outstanding achievement of the Turnovo school, exemplifying above all its distinctive departure from the idealized Byzantine style and towards the more realistic, representational forms characteristic of the Italian Renaissance. The portrait of the Tsar, particularly, has the air of having been drawn from life; contemporary sources refer to his 'smooth, nice-looking face, fine appearance and kind, direct eyes'.

The miniature shows the Royal Family in conventional hierarchical order, identified by vermillion inscriptions in Cyrillic characters carefully positioned above each portrait. The Tsar stands, with full regal insignia of sceptre and scroll, and wears a luminous red robe ('bagrenica') and boots decorated with double-headed eagles. The use of the red heraldic colour of the court of the Tsar makes clear the affinity of Bulgarian regalia with Christian solar symbolism indicating divine majesty, which is continued in the sun-shaped border of the red robe, combined with the moon-shaped border ornament, the symbol for divine wisdom. The insignia thus symbolize the Tzar's divine authority, while the inscription specifically identifies the union in him of spritual and secular power – a key element of the Orthodox medieval monarchy (*see* fig.12):

Ivan Alexander
IN CHRIST GOD FAITHFUL
Tsar and Autocrat of
all Bulgarians and Greeks

The Bulgarian imperial title 'Tsar', which replaced the old title 'Khana-syuvigy' was dramatically established by force of arms and subsequently legitimized by diplomacy after the Christianization of Bulgaria in 865 by Boris I (852–892). His son Simeon (893–927) adopted the title 'Tsar' following the establishment of

(*Opposite, above*) 9 The capture, imprisonment, execution and entombment of John the Baptist, with Herod banqueting and Salome with John the Baptist's head (f.44).

(*Opposite, below*) 10 Christ blessing the five loaves and two fishes and feeding the multitude, followed by the miracle of Christ and Peter walking on water (f.45).

КЪZКΣΕΤΝШΧΙΕΟΒΝ:

ПРΟΤΝΒΕΝЪΚΣΤΡЪ:

11 The royal portrait: Tsar Ivan Alexander and his family (ff. 2v–3).

† ѱешѡравъхаѣавѣрнаа
иновопросвѣщеннаа
црца, исамодръжица
вьсѣмь
блъгарсомь
игрькомь:

† їѡанъалеѯанⷬ
въхаⷭваⷡвѣрнⷫцрь
исамⷪдръжⷰⷲ
вьсѣⷨблъгарⷭⷩ
игрькⷭⷯⷯ

їѡ шишма
цⷬ снъ
велика цⷬ їѡ

їѡасⷩ
цⷬ
снъ
цревь

алеⷲ
за

12 Detail of the inscription above the head of Tsar Ivan Alexander (f.3).

Gospels was produced at the height of his reign, when he was probably about 55 years old, and was regarded by his subjects as 'The Good Tsar', a parallel with the Renaissance ideal of the humanist, altruistic nobleman. The Tsar's sons – Ivan Shishman, identified as 'The Tsar-son of the Great Tsar', and wearing the hereditary red robe and holding a cross-shaped sceptre and scroll, and Ivan Asen, 'Tsar-son of the Tsar', wearing an official purple Duke's robe and holding a sceptre – stand on either side of the Tsar, in order of importance. The Tsaritza Theodora, suitably portrayed in regal splendour, is identified by the inscription 'Newly Enlightened', a reference to her conversion to Christianity from Judaism. The inscription confirms that the new Tsaritsa was granted the same title as her husband, 'Autocrat over all Bulgarians and Greeks'. It was as a result of Theodora's success in ensuring the accession to the throne in 1371 of her own eldest son, Ivan Shishman, that the country was divided and subsequently fell to the Turks during his reign, marking the end of the ascendancy of the medieval Bulgarian monarchy.

The other members of the royal family are portrayed on folio 2v: Duke Constantin, the Tsar's son-in-law is depicted in the formal purple garb of the duke, next to his wife, the duchess Kera Thamara, the Tsar's eldest daughter, also in a purple robe and red mantle. Their marriage ended in divorce and Thamara, in her 30s and famous for her rare beauty was said (in a panegyric from the fourteenth-century copy of Boril's Synodic, now Bulgarian National Library N289 (55)) to have been given by her brother Ivan Shishman – then the Tsar – to the Turkish Sultan Murad (probably in 1375) as a prize for peace.

Next to her is Keratza – the Tsar's younger daughter, in the red robe and green mantle of a princess, identified simply as 'miss'. From an act of the synod of Constantinople patriarchate of 1355, regarding her betrothment to Andronicus, the Byzantine Emperor's son, it is known that her name was Maria, though her name is also recorded as Vasilisa. It therefore seems likely that, according to aristocratic tradition, she had a double name, Maria-Vasilisa. At the time she was ten years old – not unusual for a medieval royal marriage.

The portrait of Desislava, the Tsar's youngest daughter, with official robes and sceptre, completes this last dynastic portrait of medieval Bulgarian royalty, being blessed by the hand of God in striking rays of blue light.

the Bulgarian imperial Christian doctrine and of Bulgaria as a powerful player in the Balkans. The title was recognised by the Byzantine patriarch Nicolas I Mysticus after Simeon's seige of Constantinople in August 913, followed by a reception in his honour at Blachernae, the palace of Constantinople's court. In 926 Tsar Simeon became the second European ruler, after Charlemagne in 800, to have his imperial status recognised by the western theocracy of Rome.

His son Peter (927–970) succeeded in securing a reaffirmation of the Eastern theocracy by a treaty, reinforced by his marriage to the granddaughter of the Byzantine Emperor Romanus Lecapenos (920–943) – Maria-Irina – in Constantinople in 927. The final diplomatic revision of the charter was carried out in 1204 at an official coronation service in Turnovo, conducted by Pope Innocent III's envoy, Cardinal Leo, who bestowed the title of 'Rex' upon Tsar Calojan. Thus, five centuries after they had established an imperial state on the Balkans in 681, the Bulgarian tsars had received recognition of their status from the two theocratic European heads.

Ivan Alexander was the 39th ruler and 27th Tsar, reigning from 1331 to 1371. He was descended from two royal dynasties, the Terthers on his father's side, and the Assenev's, on his mother's. The portrait in the

THE GOSPELS' LATER HISTORY

The book is altogether one of the most curious monuments of bygone days to be found in any Library in Europe.

Thus the Hon. Robert Curzon (1810–1873) described the Gospels of Tsar Ivan Alexander in the catalogue of his collection. An enthusiastic collector of antiquities, he had the sort of luck that every bibliophile must dream of when the chance to acquire the Gospels presented itself to him during a visit to Mount Athos in 1837.

As early as the fifteenth century, the Mount was known in the West to possess outstanding libraries. The peninsula, with its marble summit, towering over the waters of the Aegean, had been gradually established as a sacred place from the time of the earliest Christian settlements in the age of Constantine I (274–337AD), and after the iconoclastic era, it became a particularly attractive place to settle for monks who desired a life of contemplation, prayers and mortification of the flesh. The mount's legendary purity was secured by a strict rule, approved by the Emperor Constantine IX Monomachus in 1045, barring women and female creatures of any kind from the area and, apart from the period from the late eleventh to early thirteenth centuries when the Mount was an independent monastic republic, any other visitors to the Mount required special authorisation from the Patriarch of Constantinople.

In the spring of 1837, the 23-year-old Oxford-educated Robert Curzon, armed with a letter of recommendation from the Archbishop of Canterbury and accompanied by a friend from the British Embassy in Athens, presented himself before His Holiness Patriarch Gregorios and revealed his desire to discover lost antiquities. Finding it difficult to comprehend 'how a mere Archbishop could possibly be the head of any Christian hierarchy', the Patriarch at first seemed to be about to decline Curzon's request, but he was swayed by the presence of an Embassy official and gave Curzon a letter guaranteeing his 'reception by every monastery which acknowledges the supremacy of the Orthodox faith of the Patriarch of Constantinople'.

The insular monastic community of Mount Athos had long been the theological and spiritual centre for the perpetuation of the authentic Orthodox creed and it was from here that the Hesychast doctrine had spread through the Byzantine Empire. Following the Ottoman invasion, the twenty monasteries of Mount Athos provided a safe haven for some of the most precious relics of Byzantium and the Balkans, including the Gospels of Tsar Ivan Alexander which survived in the Library of the Monastery of St Paul following its exile to safety in Moldavia.

The only clue to the manuscript's dramatic exile following the fall of Turnovo on 17 July 1393 is found on folio 2, with a note of the Gospels first move from Turnovo to Moldavia, composed in the manner of the inscription in the Royal Miniature:

The son of Voivod Stefan, Ivan Alexander, in Christ God faithful Voivod and ruler of the whole land of Moldavia, bought the Gospels which had been deposited in pledge. Let God have mercy upon him and grant him eternal life as well as long life here.

The Moldavian Ivan Alexander (1402–1432), who had evidently been fascinated by the Gospels (and possibly also by its association with his namesake), is known to have been a famous bibliophile and patron of the arts, during a period when free Christian activity was possible in the Balkans only to the north of the Danube. The Gospels' acquisition by the Voivod Ivan Alexander ensured that it was established as the hagiographic and iconographic model of the time. In the sixteenth century a further copy of it was made (now Suchevitsa 23 of the Suchava monastery), with the portraits of the Voivod's family depicted in a similar manner to the original, and the continuation of the Gospels' humanistic tradition of portraiture was assured. How the Gospels came to be 'deposited in pledge', and by whom, will probably always remain a mystery, though it seems reasonable to accept the hypothesis that the manuscript shared the fate of many Christian treasures of that time: that it was probably rescued from the destroyed town of Turnovo in 1393 and eventually brought to the safe haven of a free, neighbouring Christian country.

Several pieces of indirectly related evidence, when brought together, do suggest a possible story for the missing part of the manuscript's history. After the fall of Turnovo, a student of the prolific writer Patriarch Evtimij, Gregorij Tzamblak (died 1419), is known to have been sent by the Patriarch of Constantinople on a series of missionary visits, the first of which was to Suchava in Moldavia, from 1402–1403, where the gospel-book, Suchevitsa 23, was found. Tzamblak was the descendant of a medieval aristocratic family of Tzamblacon, renowned as military commanders, land-owners and courtiers. By virtue of his attachments to the court of Tsar Ivan Alexander and his intellectual affiliations, he may well have been in possession of the Gospels, with responsibility for rescuing it from des-truction. It is possible that he took it with him to support his initial missionary work in Moldavia, where it may have remained.

It seems likely that the later journey of the Gospels from Moldavia to Mount Athos occurred when the manuscript was made a special gift to the Bulgarian monks of the monastery of St Paul by one of the successors of the Voivod who had redeemed it from pledge. The monastery itself, for Bulgarian and Serbian monks, had been restored by Voivod Constantine Blankbanu-Hospodar of Wallachia (1688–1714). When Robert Curzon visited it more than a century later, it was still remarkably prosperous:

I was received with cheerful hospitality and soon made the acquaintance of four monks who among them spoke English, French, Italian and German . . . I saw that these books were taken care of, so I did not much like to ask whether they would part with them; more especially as the community was evidently a prosperous one, and had no need to sell their properties.

Robert Curzon; ibid.

Among the books examined by Curzon the Gospels of Tsar Ivan Alexander made an immediate impact:

The Serbian and Bulgarian manuscripts amounted about 200. . . The third manuscript was likewise a folio of the Gospel in the ancient Bulgarian language and like the other two, in uncial letters. The manuscript was quite full of illuminations from beginning to end. I had seen no book like it anywhere in the Levant, and I almost tumbled off the steps on which I was perched on the discovery of so extraordinary a volume.

Curzon later admits his astonishment, therefore, when he was offered a memento of this visit, and recorded with care his charming and witty response:

If you do not care what book it is that you are so good as to give me, let me take one which pleases me: and so saying I took down the illuminated folio of the Bulgarian gospels, and I could hardly believe I was awake when the agoumenos [the Superior of the monastery] gave it into my hands.

The manuscript remained in Curzon's private library at Parham Park until 19 April 1876 when his son, Robin, 15th Baron Zouche, deposited his collection on perma-nent loan to the British Museum. It was officially bequeathed to the Museum in 1917, by Darea, 16th Baroness Zouche. At that time the collection numbered 284 volumes, including printed books and 128 oriental manuscripts; Curzon himself had previously recorded his valuation of his collection on f.2v of his catalogue (now British Library Additional MS 64098) as £5000 Sterling. The Gospels of Tsar Ivan Alexander was separately valued at £1000, an indication of its relative importance and value.

Curzon's stroke of astonishing good fortune may well have saved the manuscript from destruction in a devastating fire which swept through the Library of the monastery of St Paul in 1905. It ensured that this unique monument to the 'inner holy word', created by anony-mous Turnovo artists, can still be seen today on display in The British Library.

THE MANUSCRIPT

The Scribe and Script

Cyrillic Script

The Gospels of Tsar Alexander is written in Bulgarian, in the Cyrillic script, and was the work of a single scribe who signed himself 'Simonŭ' in the colophon on f.275. The same hand had probably earlier contributed to the Chronicle of Manasses (now Vatican MS, Slav. 2); the calligraphic style of both manuscripts reflects the same formal, confident handling of uncial Cyrillic.

The Cyrillic alphabet descended from the Glagolitic script, created by St Constantine-Cyril, the philosopher of Thessalonica (827–869) in 855, and is believed to have been modelled on the phonetic framework of south-western Bulgaria. The Cyrillic was also compiled with elements drawn from the Greek majuscule (uncial), an endeavour associated with the school of St Cyril, his brother St Methodius and their disciples. Under the patronage of the first Christian Tsar of Bulgaria, Boris (852–889), St Cyril's disciple Naum founded the school of Preslav, while another disciple, Clement, established one in the western centre of Ochrid. The latter was a phenomenal educational undertaking, admitting 3500 students during its first seven years, following the collapse of the mission to Moravia and the expulsion of St Cyril's disciples in c.885 and the return of a group of them to Bulgaria. The double scribal tradition flourished into the tenth century under Tsar Simeon (reigned 893–927): the Cyrillic was favoured as a popular educational vehicle, later used in missionary work in the Kievan principality, Wallachia and Moldavia, while the Glagolitic script maintained its sacred status as the first western vernacular to bear the Holy Word alongside Latin, Greek and Hebrew (a fact recognised in the West as early as the sixteenth century by Martin Luther). Several old Bulgarian manuscripts from both scribal traditions have come down to us from the tenth century.

The earliest Cyrillic text is dated from 993 AD – a funerary inscription executed on the orders of the Bulgarian Tsar Samuel (976–1014), found in the village of Djerman. The Cyrillic uncial of the Gospels of Tsar Ivan Alexander is the finest palaeographic specimen, representing the climax of the script's development, during which time Byzantine gospel-books were predominantly written in minuscule (gradually, from the tenth century onwards) and the production of gospels in uncial became a characteristically Balkan practice. The Gospels of Tsar Ivan Alexander is marked up with lectionary signs and was probably intended for display and regular use in Ivan Alexander's Patriarchate Church on Tsarevetz during grand feast-day services attended by the Tsar.

Scripts in the Manuscript

The scribe Simeon demonstrated his calligraphic skills in three forms of writing: ornamented initials, gold initials and formal uncial, begun on the first pages of each gospel in gold and continued in black. The scribe and artists appear to have worked in close collaboration. The frameless miniatures display an organic unity with the text, their area and position no doubt calculated in advance, observing the working page area produced by horizontal lines (23–25) and vertical lines (6), probably inscribed with a bone knife. The structure of the overall design is based on a standard system in which the uncial letter-form represents one unit or module to which the other elements relate in ratio: 1 (uncial letter): 3 (gold initial): 10 (ornamented initial and miniature): 30 (headpiece): 50 (text block): 65 (folio). The effect is of a fully integrated composition. Where there are accidental errors, corrections have been made so that they do not affect the text structure (for example, fig.35), and when a miniature is too high, the extended part is drawn in the margin (for example, fig.50).

The single-column text, placed between the second and third vertical lines of the page, is in a standard formal uncial: upright writing fixed on the baseline with well-maintained consistency of size and distance between the letters. The text is obviously considered as an aesthetic vehicle in its own right, as every opportunity for decoration has been taken – calligraphically

13 Headpiece of the Gospel of St Luke (f.137).

14 Headpiece of the Gospel of St Matthew (f.6).

elaborated strokes, ligatures, abbreviations, accents and certain marginal signs, in a quite extensive, uninterrupted flow of words. Semi-colons are frequently used after text preceding a miniature, as though the illumination is a pictorial quotation of the narrative (fig. 1).

The semi-uncial writing is of two types – one more formal, in faded red, with standard letter shaping, employed in the Menologion (the full calendar of grand feast days) and some marginal text, similar to the writing of the 'magic square', and an informal, more angular script in brighter red, employed in the Synaxaria and the rest of the marginal additions.

The gold initials of the titles of each gospel and the section titles are beautifully handled and epitomise the opportunities for variation of the design provided by the shape and sequence of the letters. Some letters are written superscript, while others (most commonly the letter O) incorporate the next character within their inner space (figs 13, 14). A technical feature common to both the miniatures and the gold initials is the yellow gesso which seems to have been applied under the gold of both (*see* page 33).

The inscriptions on the royal portraits (*see* fig. 11) have been made distinctive with the use of vermilion ink, the traditional heraldic royal red. Each inscription begins with a stylised cross and runs in a symmetrical pattern. That of the royal family on f. 2v forms a sloping rectangle, while the inscriptions for the Tsar and Tsaritsa (f. 3) are displayed in broken lines, making full use of the space around them as an organic part of the design.

The scribe has also skilfully continued the vibrating effect of the decorative elements of the headpieces in the ornamented initials. At the head of St Matthew's Gospel the letter K is particularly solid and heavily decorated, presenting the most diverse ornamental vocabulary of all the major initials, with knot and flower motif interleaving patterns (fig. 14). The Z-shape at the beginning of St Mark's Gospel (fig. 30) allows a more delicate combination of a knot and other interwoven patterns. The simple initial P from the Gospel of St Luke (fig. 13) matches the geometrical pattern of the headpiece, while the elegant and solid V of St John's Gospel (frontispiece) is used against a predominantly flowery pattern on a huge gold ground, to begin the opening sentence 'In the beginning was the word'. The clear decorative similarity between the initials and the headpieces suggests that the scribe worked on both, though not, presumably, on the portraits contained in the headpieces.

The 'Magic Square'

The Gospels provides a unique example of the orthodox 'nomina sacra', a 'magic square', which serves as a mark of ownership and offers evidence of the historical and spiritual status of the manuscript (half-title page). The magic square's representation of the name of the Tsar in various coded ways is a rare attempt to create a type of palindrome of ownership. The square, on folio 273v of the manuscript, is divided into 625 smaller squares, to accommodate the 24 letters, arranged in rhombuhedral symmetry. The first twelve rhombus patterns, starting at the centre, create a blooming effect of repeated initials, while the other twelve produce a closing effect, resting in the corners. In the centre itself is inscribed the name of the Tsar in the standard abbreviated formula, IV, from which all codes of reading the square emanate.

The codes for reading the magic square apply in three main ways, revealing the words *Io Alexander Tsarya Tetravaggel* – The Four Gospels of Tsar Ivan Alexander. The first code reads in the form of a cross, starting from the centre and moving outwards to the four corners and then turning to left or right, revealing the full text eight times. The second operates according to the orientation of the four sections of the cross-divided square. For example, the upper right section reads from the centre up and to the right in a zigzag pattern. The third code allows reading from the centre towards any corner, assuming you move one letter at a time, reading outwards on a rhombuhedral line. This collage-like pattern has a vibrating effect, as if the words are sparkling out of the initials 'IV' in the centre. The letters are written in pale wine-red pigment also used in the narrow decorative border which surrounds the square, while the three central vertical and horizontal lines are flaked with gold to form a subtle cross. The letters are written in the same formal style as the rest of the manuscript; since the scribe Simeon states in his colophon that he wrote 'this manuscript' it is possible that he was also the inventor of the magic square (although since he does not make specific mention of this unique feature, it is equally possible that is was the contribution of a learned court official).

This type of sacred writing seems to have been a well-established art in the Turnovo School. Three similar examples appear in an early fourteenth-century manuscript produced at Turnovo, the Norov Psalter (Moscow GIM, Uvar. N285). The first is a simple one-word example, but the other two create four-word sentences with eulogistic epithets dedicated to God and the psalter. Their presence supports the assumption that the art of creating palindromes was cultivated by the scribes and monks within the Turnovo school.

In Christian art this curious device, originally known as 'technopaignion' or the 'art game', was first employed in the fourth century by the court poet of Constantine the Great, Publius Optatianus, who was said to have cast some of his panegyric poems within outlines ('carmina figurata'), in the form of crosswords. From that time the Christogramme was established as a representative symbol of Christ, an example of Constantine's interest in the idea of 'cult without image'. Also part of the 'nomina sacra' system are the 'poems by figure' popular in Carolingian and Ottonian art where the complex reading code is indicated only by occasional use of colour and where mirrors are sometimes needed to abstract the correct reading. A later parallel can be drawn with Elizabethan magic tables designed to create a state of perfection through the invocation and multiplication of God's names written in geometric patterns. The archetype most probably dates back to the Greek magic rolls, an example of which can be found in Oslo University Library (P. Oslo I ivc), the most richly illustrated Greek papyrus ever found. It contains a picture of a mythical demon inscribed with letters in vertical and horizontal sequences, believed to have had some magic significance.

The magic square completes the structure of the Gospels and the scribe Simeon's learned scheme, which began with the royal portraits, continued with a portrait of the Tsar at the climax of its story (the last judgement) and concludes with the palindrome of the Tsar's ownership. This cycle can thus be seen as a representation of the Bulgarian concept of regal power: majesty – the royal portrait; political power – the last judgement; religious law – the presentation scenes; magic – the magic square.

The Artists of the Gospels

In Orthodox iconography the anonymity of the artist is an important indication of his humility before the Almighty and most works produced in medieval Byzantine and Balkan scriptoria are unsigned. The Gospels of Tsar Ivan Alexander is no exception to this tradition, but, most unusually, the scribe Simeon refers in the colophon to 'artists', making clear that the manuscript was the work of several hands:

With bright colours and gold, artists decorated the work artistically for the glory of their Kingdom.

Gospels of Tsar Ivan Alexander, f.274

The Iconographic Background

The Orthodox artist inherited clearly defined values which encouraged self-denial, with the aim of ensuring that the viewer or reader focused directly on the content of the image itself, or even beyond it:

We do not adore the colours and the art, but the type of Christ – the real person of Christ – who is in the Heavens; for, says St Basil, the homage rendered to an image belongs to the model of that image.

Didron, M., *Christian Iconography*, London, 1886, vol.II, p.394

This was the teaching of ancient tradition, systematically recorded in the earliest surviving Byzantine guide for painters, the *Hermeneia* or *Painter's Manual*, compiled by the monk Dionysius of Phourna, *c*.1730–34, purportedly drawing on the works of Manuel Panselinus (early fourteenth century) who, Dionysius claimed, was considered the Giotto of the Byzantine School (though his claims have since been debated). The fact that works such as the Gospels were the joint effort of several collaborators within a scriptorium, and accorded with the traditions of the Orthodox school which ensured that archaic models were perpetuated, denied the painters even the same rights as the scribes who could at least make reference to their contribution to the work. Instead, there were strict prerequisites for approaching the science of painting which included 'belief in God and the piety in art', considered as a Divine attribute; fear of God; and a prayer to Christ submitted at the icon of the Virgin 'Hodegetria', or guide. The artist should then 'work without reflection'. Another popular set of instructions in Giotto's scriptorium, recorded in the fifteenth century by Cennino Cennini, a student of a son of a Giotto disciple, was similarly based on 'Enthusiasm, Reverence, Obedience and Constancy', with

(*Left*)
15 Christ teaching
(f.58).

(*Below, centre*)
16 Christ teaching
(f.231v).

(*Left*)
17 The Resurrection:
Christ descending
into Hell and freeing
Adam and Eve (f.85).

(*Opposite, above*)
18 The Resurrection:
Christ descending
into Hell and freeing
Adam and Eve
(f.133).

(*Opposite, below*)
19 Christ appears to
Mary and two angels
on the tomb after the
Resurrection (f.269).

28

И МИНЖВШИСЪ БОТЪ · МАРИА МАГДАЛЫ
НИ · ИЛАРІА ІАКОВЛѢ · И САЛОМИ, КОУПИ

ЩМОУ ТЕННИКОМ БЫ ІАКО ВИД ВЪ ТѢ ГАН
С НАРЕЧЕ ЕН :

СЪ Щ ОУ ЖЕ ПОЗДѢ ВЪ ДНЬ ТЪ · ВЪ ЕДИ
НЖ СЖ БОТЖ · И ДВЕРЕМЪ ЗАТВОРЕНО

20 Christ praying in the Garden of Gethsemene, returning to the sleeping disciples and waking them (f.127).

strict prescriptions for personal discipline 'in the interest of decorum'.

The accumulation of artistic experience during the post-iconoclastic period collected in Dionysius' manual reflects a long-developed sacred tradition, revealed only in the nineteenth century when M. Didron discovered the manual on Mount Athos:

The work, the date of which in its original form is unknown, has been extended and completed in successive centuries . . . it had been loaded with notes, written by the artist and his master, which notes, in due course of time would be incorporated with the book, when recopied, just as those earlier ones, found by the painters of the fifteenth and sixteenth centuries on the margins of their books had been incorporated in the work by them. And so this book grew from century to century and year to year. A transcript of this Guide is to be found in every Atelier in Mount Athos . . .

Didron, M., *Christian Iconography*, London, 1886, vol.II, pp.190–191

The Turnovo School

The art of the Gospels of Ivan Alexander belongs to this tradition and reflects the close relations which the Tsar cultivated with Mount Athos. The fourteenth-century Turnovo revival derived direct inspiration from the spiritual school of Mount Athos. Its leader, Theodosij (died 1363), was a dedicated disciple of the Holy Mount, who propagated the Hesychast ideology at the monastery of Kilifarevo near Turnovo, and was the spiritual adviser to Ivan Alexander. It was the advanced literary

activities of the Bulgarian monks from Zographou monastery on Mount Athos which fashioned the Bulgarian language reforms of the fourteenth century, sanctioned by the then patriarch of Turnovo, Evtimij, a disciple of Theodosij. The spirit of these literary reforms, which included the revival of the classic literary style of the school of Saints Cyril and Methodius, embellished with contemporary touches, was similar to that of the artistic revival which enlivened the canon with colourful local elements, developing a distinctively Bulgarian style.

This tendency dates back to 1259 and the art of Boyana church near Sofia, built under the patronage of the Turnovo nobleman, Calojan. Here the story of Christ, and representations of martyrs and saints, are depicted alongside portraits of the then Tsar Constantine-Asen and Tsaritsa Irina, Calojan himself and his wife Desislava. The artistic challenge – to find an accessible way of presenting religious subjects – was met through the exploration of human aspects of the stories depicted; through use of a new palette of saturated colours; through the artists' technical skills which enabled a more realistic treatment of the figures; and by the use of frieze composition. This created a new artistic formula, nurtured in thirteenth-century Turnovo while Constantinople was under the control of the crusaders, which made a valuable contribution to the artistic heritage of Ivan Alexander's reign. Works of the Turnovo school reveal the development of the Boyana formula in the art of their miniatures, continuing the exploration of human aspects of religious imagery combined with a variety of artistic innovations. The Turnovo school also shared stylistic affinities with the

(*Above*) 21 Christ preaching (f.154v).

(*Right*) 22 Christ and his disciples; a turning point in the style of the illustrations (f.156).

(*Below*) 23 (*left*), 24 (*right*) The parable of the tree, and birds nesting there (ff.177v and 180v).

(*Above, top*)
25 The parable of the fig tree (f.179v).

(*Above, centre*)
26 John the Baptist baptising people on the River Jordon (f.12).

27 Details showing the two principle techniques and styles: (*top*) John the Evangelist (f.272v); (*bottom*) John the Baptist (f.12).

(*Left*)
28 St John baptising Jesus on the River Jordan (f.13).

early fourteenth-century works of Pancelinus on Mount Athos, who was renowned for the excellence of his portraiture and his treatment of posture and quality of movement. Both the Turnovo and Mount Athos schools also shared the practice of blending succeeding scenes into continuous units, rather than framing them individually. The Gospels of Tsar Ivan Alexander offers many fine examples of all of these features.

The Art of the Gospels

A close study of the 367 miniatures in the Gospels reveals a homogenous and regular linear style, an essential simplicity of detail and a subtle expressiveness developed within the standard modular structure which produced an integral harmony. The skills of the miniaturists are notable for their integrity, and the portraiture in particular, with its elaborate linear modelling and delicate use of colour, is of a rare standard. As the product of variations of this style, including miniatures of many types, from small single frameless ones (fig.66) to larger compressed friezes (fig.9) and full pages (fig.58), the manuscript is a fine example of how the artists within one scriptorium approached the search for aesthetic and spiritual integrity within the mature Palaeologan style which was already beginning to exhibit stereotypical features. The effect of this style is that the images move away from the ceremonial, mannerist grandeur usually favoured in Byzantine art, as the richness of movement and life within the narrative become dominant and are executed with immediacy and plasticity, yet preserving their spiritual significance (*see* figs 7, 11, 27, 36 and 59).

This combination of a more realistic and subtle approach testifies to the finest artistic intuition at work in the creation of the Gospels' miniatures; thus the manuscript can be considered a highly original work of art, the illuminators as artists as much as craftsmen.

Examination of the miniatures under a microscope, and under various lights, reveals some of the artists' technical secrets, and serves as a means of identifying the individuals at work. Two dominant styles reveal, in varying degrees, both the conservative impact of the Byzantine tradition and the innovation of the Turnovo school. The archaic tradition is exemplified by simple gradations in tone, fixed in irregular, linear modelling painted directly onto the surface of the vellum, which serves to pick out the highlights in a miniature. The palette is reduced to a range of clear, dense and darker brown tones, without the customary Byzantine variations of gradual tonal shifts, which leaves each brushstroke distinct and clearly visible and gives the form greater graphic prominence. This minimalist approach is seen particularly in figs 16, 22, 26 and 44, in the miniatures after f.155 in the Gospel of St Luke, and consistently in the illuminations of the Gospel of John. Some of the miniatures produced using this technique are also notable for their weaker resistance to the effects of time and damaging conditions. Some have faded, presumably through drying out, as it is obvious that in most cases no substance has been used to ensure sufficient impregnation of the vellum with the paints (for example in fig.60).

The second technique presents the reverse process, in which the gradation of tones is built up on a pinkish ground (a borrowing from the Byzantine 'couleur changant' technique) and the highlights of faces are executed by superimposing striking white strokes. The palette here includes brighter colours (the use of red is particularly notable) with receding black and brown shadows finished with gold, and gold for red. The brush work is more experimental, with more juxtaposed strokes creating an impressionistic effect (*see* figs 10, 11, 21, 27, and 36). Most of the miniatures of the Gospel of St Matthew (except ff.7v–9 and 10v–13), the Gospel of St Mark and the Gospel of St Luke up to f.154 are the result of exploring this type of technique. Most of the miniatures are distinguished by their remarkably good condition which seems to have been achieved through the use of an oily substance, traces of which can be seen on the vellum in the case of the best preserved miniatures, sometimes even offset onto the next folio. A curious recipe for ensuring durability and brilliance survives in Dionysius's *Painters' Manual*, which includes virgin sesame oil, essence of garlic and shell powder to produce: 'a brilliant effect of the brush'. For the gilded parts candle grease tallow, gall, mercury, the famous ochra of Constantinople, the white of an egg and, finally, distilled raki were used. After being applied to the parchment the gilding was left to dry in the shade and then had to be burnished with the careful rubbing of a volcanic stone so that the brilliance achieved by the painting on it could stand comparison only with ' the moon in all its splendour'. A similar, and possibly less smelly, recipe was circulating amongst western artists, along with the specific instruction that the artist should first get the stone nice and warm before burnishing by clasping it to his bosom.

Within the first technique mentioned, one stylistic

variety developed which simplified the schematic formula in a peculiarly archaic manner, resulting in minimal lines, simple colouring (figs 26, 37 (centre) and 63) and – occasionally – the foreshortening of proportions (fig. 24). Within the second technique are two coordinated artistic variations. The first is an example of the flat, early ecclesiastical style, with a controlled rendering of elongated proportions (figs 1, 4 and 5); the second testifies to the Renaissance humanist influence in religious art, preserving its linear elegance while intensifying the modelling and the colouring to give volume and perspective and creating a more tangible, representational effect in some particularly fine portraiture (figs 11, 37 and title-page). There are three distinct variations discernible in the depiction of Jesus' face: long and pale, with a serene countenance (figs 16, 22 and 24); long and lively with a majestic expression (figs 5, 20 and 55); and natural, oval and lively with a vigorous and immediate expression (figs 15, 21 and 58).

On the basis of this study, the participation of three principal masters in the artistic creation of the Gospels can be identified. The spirit of this collaboration is dominated by the pictorial style of the artist whom we will call the Renaissance master; he was endowed with the supreme talent and produced the masterpiece of the manuscript, the Royal portrait (front cover and fig. 11); the final scenes of the Gospels – the Tsar with the Evangelists (figs 32, 33 and title-page), the scene of the Last Judgement (fig. 58), and the Adoration of the Magi (fig. 37). In this last miniature is a radical compositional change which imbues the ecclesiastical overtones of the illustration with humanistic significance and realism, a feature of the composition perpetuated in later orthodox art (*see* p. 62).

The second master, while adopting in moderation the Renaissance master's technique and realism, adhered to the normative ecclesiastical scheme, preserving the flat style, from a ground-level perspective considered essential for the portrayal of holy images and betraying the ultimate ecclesiastical type of reverence. His contribution appears regularly in the treatment of the genealogy of Christ, the Parables and the Passion cycles of the first two gospels (figs 1, 4 and 5).

The third master, presumably of the older generation, remained the conservative force of monastic spirituality, modified now to serve the introverted Hesychast ideology, resulting in ascetic imagery which is a vehicle for theology rather than aesthetic. The remote foreshortened figures betray the use of a perspective from above, as if the artist imagined the world seen from a heavenly viewpoint. This, along with the use of an opaque style, made further remote with still tones, reveals the highest monastic ideal of spiritual, wholesome reverence. This artist worked on the beginning of the story of Jesus' incarnation (figs 35 and 37 (centre)), on the baptism of Jesus (fig. 28) and elsewhere in the gospels of Luke and John. This archaic style is similar to that in a contemporary manuscript of the Turnovo School, the Tomic Psalter, in which the depiction of the old shepherd in the principal Nativity scene is remarkably similar to that of the Nativity in the Gospel of St Matthew.

Beyond these differences, simplicity transcends all three styles, and while architectural and rocky backgrounds are still rendered symbolically – in the usual brown and green decorative scheme – the treatment of drapery is very elaborate. Highlights have been secured by the use of receding angular lines. Vegetation and birds are carefully drawn, in traditional style, and are particularly impressive (figs 23, 24, 25 and 56), as is the amount of observation of realistic detail overall – children climbing trees (f. 59) or perched on their parents' shoulders (fig. 53), or the marriage feast at Cana packed with the elements of daily life (fig. 47).

The three masters also seem to have worked together on individual scenes and their collaboration can be discerned in varying combinations, for example in the manuscript's opening pages: fig. 11 – the Renaissance master; fig. 4 – the joint work of the Renaissance Master and his follower, the second master; fig. 1 – the second master; fig. 37 – the Renaissance master's hand again, with the archaic master.

Within the three types of style less effective contributions can also be distinguished, in various combinations, indicating the likely involvement of disciples of the three masters as assistants and decorators. This is particularly noticeable when comparing works on identical subjects, such as fig. 35 in contrast with fig. 37, figs 26 and 28, figs 45 and 46, and figs 17 and 18. The work of assistants or disciples can be discerned where a mixed technique results in conventional colouring or a corrupt decorative scheme (figs 40, 41 and 63), as well as in inferior proportions and less effective portraiture (for example in figs 16, 35, 46 and 52). By involving both masters and pupils as part of a special, monumental project from the capital's principal scriptorium, the Gospels reveals the richness of the school's traditions and the diversity of its humanistic endeavour and innovation. In this context, the phenomenally short period in which the Gospels was created – between 1355–1356, at the rate of one miniature per day – begins

29 The construction of the 'golden mean' employed in the royal portrait (240 × 385mm), (ff.2v–3).

to seem a more realistic timetable.

The testimony for a collaborative creative discipline existing within the fourteenth-century Turnovo school is found in the scribe Simeon's colophon, where he reveals how the Turnovo artists implemented St Basil's key teaching on the perception of holy images, in accordance with the major Hesychast principle of 'the inner light', as their creative manifesto:

This life-given source of the New Blessing and the New Beatitudes of the sweet teaching of Jesus, the God's Messiah, was created to transmit the Four Gospels, and not simply for the outward beauty of its decoration, of colours, gold, precious stones, and diamonds, but primarily to express the inner Divine word, the revelation and the sacred vision.

The Gospels of Tsar Ivan Alexander, f.274

The Royal Portrait

The major artistic achievement of the Gospels, the portrait of the Tsar and his family, reveals how Bulgarian and Byzantine portraiture drew upon an artistic tradition dating back to the early sixth century with the mosaics of the Emperor Justinian and Empress Theodora in the church of St Vitale, Ravenna, then at the western tip of the Byzantine empire. Similar mosaics and wall paintings became a common sight in Orthodox churches in the post-iconolastic era. The eleventh-century mosaics of the Emperor John II Comnenus and Empress Irene, and of the Emperor Constantine IX Monomachus and Empress Zöe in the Hagia Sofia church in Constantinople, the thirteenth-century frescoes of the Bulgarian Tsar Constantine and Tsaritsa Irina, and of Duke Calojan and his wife Desislava in the Boyana church near Sofia, and the fourteenth-century wall paintings of the Serbian King Stefan Dušan with his wife Elena and son Urosh in Lesnova church, are all examples of the proto-Renaissance type of formal and stylised portraiture which constituted the

35

Byzantine-Balkan tradition of authority and majesty.

The fourteenth-century humanist movement reintroduced the art of portraiture into manuscript illumination, earlier exemplified in the portrait of the Bulgarian Tsar Boris I in the Pedagogic Gospel of the eleventh century (now in a twelfth-century copy in Moscow, CIM, 262); and in the portrait of the Byzantine Emperor Nicephoros III Botaniates (1078–81) in the homilies of St John Chrysostom (Paris, Bibliothèque Nationale, MS Coislin grec 79). This trend was already advanced in historical illumination: in a twelfth-century chronicle by Nicetas Choniates (Vienna Cod. Hist. gr. 53) both kings and common people are vividly depicted in historical scenes.

In 1345 a translation of the Latin *History of Troy* by Guido della Colonne was added to the Turnovo copy of the Byzantine chronicle of Manasses, along with a lavishly illustrated text on Bulgarian history where Bulgarian monarchs are depicted in a variety of action scenes. The classicized Bulgarian version is reminiscent of works of the Italian Renaissance in its return to classical sources and ideas (the portrait of Tsar Ivan Alexander in this work is explicitly compared with Alexander the Great).

In the royal portrait of the Gospels the Turnovo Master has achieved a new humanistic solution to the traditional Byzantine hagiographic formula which required a predominance of 'essence' over 'substance'. While perpetuating certain formal iconographic elements – the symmetry, forward facing and fine linear modelling – he has undertaken a radical change in the treatment of faces and of the background. By abandoning canonical borders, panels and heavy gold ground, he allows an individual expressive vigour to emanate from the modelling of features, particularly in the hands and eyes, with a simple and yet striking effect, while the skilful use of bright colours creates the impression of a radiant space. As a result the portrait style embodies the Renaissance maxim 'Man is a measure of all things' (*see* p.20).

The design of the composition in the form of a colonnade conforms with another classical principle, that of the 'golden mean'. It provides a structure to the portrait, coordinating the eight images and inscriptions into an integrated whole, invested with proportions traditionally representing the universal unity attributed by christians to the son of God (fig.29). The portrait illustrates how cogent the iconographic figurative scheme could be, drawing upon classical tradition, yet introducing its own sources of inspiration.

The Headpieces

The Turnovo artists' treatment of the headpieces is the most conservative element of the Gospels' illumination. Though the headpieces themselves serve a purely decorative function, the Evangelists within the headpieces are depicted, in the manner of a classical opening, as the authors of the Gospels, a common feature of Byzantine art. The artist of the four headpieces has incorporated the portraits of the four Evangelists – Matthew, Mark, Luke and John – into medallions, within elaborate decorative schemes comprising some of the most complex designs in the Gospels. Within the circular ornaments of the first headpiece, the portrait of St Matthew in the central medallion shows him, in traditional style, as an old man contemplating the gospel he has copied. He is identified by an abbreviated description in gold. In five smaller medallions, symmetrically arranged around him, are portraits of some Old Testament characters. The top one is identified with the heading 'the ancient of days' and two six-wing cherubim are placed on either side, while Abraham and Isaac are shown in the lower medallions, all relating to the genealogy of Christ at the beginning of St Matthew's Gospel (fig.14).

In the Gospel of St Mark (fig.30), the Old Testament characters are gradually abandonned, with St Mark shown copying the gospel from a roll in the central medallion, surrounded by Christ, John the Baptist and the prophet Isiah. Again the design continues the circular pattern, in another skilful arrangement.

In the headpiece of the Gospel of St Luke (fig.13), the artist has created a vertical arrangement of the three medallions, the central one occupied by St Luke, traditionally depicted as a young man absorbed in the minute action of dipping his quill into his ink-pot. Christ is bestowing a blessing in the top medallion, while the lower one is dedicated to the prophet Zachariah.

The headpiece of the Gospel of St John (frontispiece) depicts the unity of the Holy Trinity, with a triple portrayal of God – God, the Son, shown as a young man; God, the Father, shown as an old man; and God, the Spirit, represented by Christ as a young child – in another imaginatively constructed circular design. Dominated by the careful portrait of St John in the central medallion, the very fine portraiture of this headpiece, clearly visible under a microscope, suggests that it is the work of the principal Renaissance master.

(*Opposite*) 30 Headpiece of the Gospel of St Mark (f.88).

Не прѣ просвѣ м Зачало еѵⷢ҇лїа

88

Єѵⷢ҇гелїє ст҃оє ѿ Марка

Зачало еѵⷢ҇лиꙗ і҃у х҃ва с҃на б҃на · ꙗко
же єсть писано въ прⷪ҇рцѣхъ · се
посылаю агг҃ла моєго прѣд ли
цемь твоимъ · иже оуготовить
пѫть твои прѣд тобою · гласъ
вопиющаго въ поустыни · оуготова
ите пѫть г҃нь, правы творите ст

31 Christ appears to his disciples after the Resurrection (*above*) and St Matthew presenting his Gospel to Tsar Ivan Alexander (f.86v).

НАНЕДЖЖНЫХРЖКЫВЪЗЛОЖЖТЪН
ЗДРАВНБЖДЖТЪ · ГЪЖЕЇСПОГЛАНН
НГОЕЖЕКЪННМЪ · ВЪЗНЕСЕСМНАНЕ
БЕСА.НСЋДЕШДЕСНЖХБА · ОННЖЕН
ШЕДШЕПРОПОВЋДААХЖ
ВЬСЖДОУ · ГЪУПОСПЋШЬ
СТВОУЖЩОУ · НСЛОВОУТВРЪ
ЖДАЖЩОУ · ПОСЛЋСТВОУЖ
ЦННЛ҇АНЗНАМЕННМН.АМННЪ:

32 The Ascension of Christ (*above*) and St Mark presenting his Gospel to Tsar Ivan Alexander (f.134v).

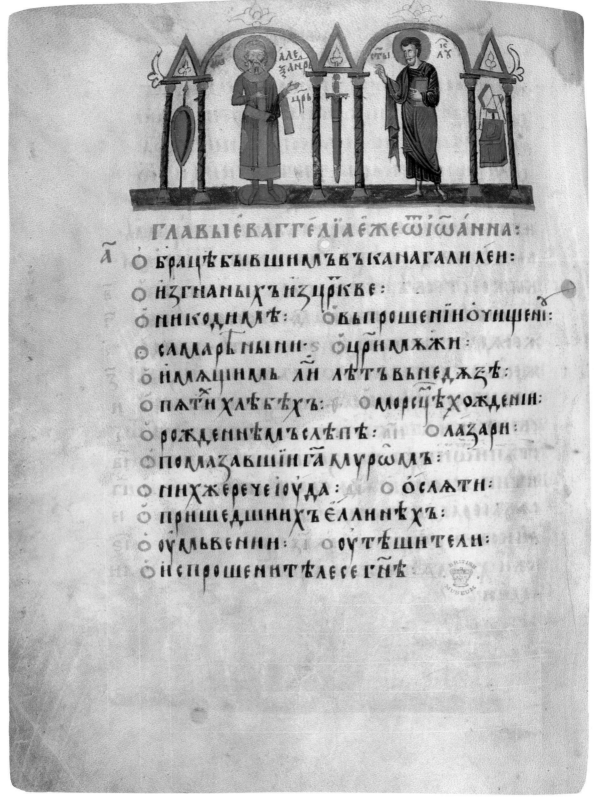

ГЛАВЫ ЕВАГГЕЛІА ѤЖЕ Ѿ ЇѠ́АННА :·

а҃ О БРАЦѢ БЫВШИМЪ ВЪ КАНА ГАЛИЛЕН :·

О НЗГНАНЫХЪ НЗ ЦРКВЕ :·

О НИКОДИМѢ :·   О ВЪПРОШЕНІ ОУНЩЕНІ :·

О САМАРѢНЫНН :·   О ЦРИ МЛЖН :·

О ИМАЩИМЪ ЛИ ЛѢТЪ ВЪ НЕДЖѢ :·

О ПѦТН ХЛѢ БѢХЪ :·   О МОРСЦѢ ХОЖДЕНІН :·

О РОЖДЕННѢМЪ СЛѢПѢ :· О ЛАЗАРН :·

О ПОМАЗАВШІН ГА МУРѠМЪ :·

О НИХЖЕ РЕЧЕ ІОУДА :·   О СЛѦТН :·

О ПРИШЕДШИНХЪ ЕЛЛИНѢХЪ :·

О ОУМЛЬВЕННН :·   О ОУТѢШНТЕЛН :·

О НСПРОШЕННН ТѢЛЕСЕ Г҃НѢ

33 St Luke presenting his Gospel to Tsar Ivan Alexander (f.212v).

Even on such a small scale the portraits of the evangelists display a variety of countenances and postures, with skilfully draped robes, particularly noticeable in the portraits of Luke and John. The effect is further enhanced with sensitive highlights and a fine finish. It is tempting to explore the idea that, while accomplishing in the headpieces this most conservative element of Byzantine art, the stillness of their background reflects the underlying unchanging wisdom of the narratives of the parables. This type of headpiece, with inscribed portraits, is a survival of a common eleventh-century style. The headpieces of the Gospels of Tsar Ivan Alexander are a new development from this style. The elaborate decorative scheme, with the use of bright and uniform colours on a gold ground, in contrast to the plain surface of the background to the portraits in the medallions, creates the effect of stained glass, nicely distinguished from the popular, fluid style.

The representation of the Evangelists as scribes is carried through from the headpieces to the illustration of the presentation of the Gospels to their patron. This portrait of Ivan Alexander duly acknowledges the union of spiritual and secular authority vested in the monarch, by contrast with earlier representations of this scene in the eleventh-century Byzantine Gospels (Paris, Bibliothèque Nationale, MS grec 74), which shows the Gospels being received by an abbot. Matthew and John are shown standing between trees, while Luke's (fig. 33) and Mark's (fig. 32) presentations are placed under a heavenly symbol – the arch – associating them with the previous ascension scenes. The presentation of the Gospels of St Mark, with its unfinished arch and simplified colouring, is the exception among the fine painterly rendering of the other three illustrations. In Luke's presentation picture the conventional attributes of shield, spear and sword for the Tsar and a lectern for the scribe, are shown. The careful modelling and fine portraiture culminate in the presentation illustration of St John's Gospel, the Tsar's patron saint, where the expressive qualities of motion, gesture and glance, indicate the hand of the Renaissance master at work.

The Life of Christ and Miracles Cycles

The usual cycle of illustration of the Orthodox bible traditionally comprises a set of 76 scenes from the life of Christ, providing a summary of the events of his life as recounted in the four gospels. The 150 miniatures in the Gospels provide a more thorough illustration of the story of the life of Christ and a double account of the

34 The Annunciation: the angel and Mary at the fountain (f. 139v).

miracle subjects. The illumination of the subject of Christ's incarnation which begins with the miniature depicting the annunciation is found only in the Gospel of St Luke (fig. 34). Mary is depicted approached by the angel at a fountain, in a simple and expressive gesture of surprise. The depiction of the scene indoors occurred in later art; this is one of the earliest apocryphal scenes adopted in Christian art. The presentation of the subject is neither ambitious nor innovative, but it does serve as a good example of the archaic simplicity which underlies all the artistic styles present in the manuscript, transcending details of individual craftsmanship.

Dionysius's *Painters' Manual* is precise on the point of the composition of the key event of the story, the nativity, reflecting (at a much later date) the traditional iconographic elements which had developed and become established well before the fourteenth century and on which the Turnovo artist would have drawn:

A grotto. Within, upon the right, the Virgin kneeling, she lays Christ, an infant in swaddling clothes, in a cradle. To the left Joseph upon his knees his hands crossed upon his breast. Behind the cradle an ox and an ass are watching. Behind the holy family are the shepherds, each holding his staff and watching with astonishment. Outside the cave, are sheep and shepherds, one of them playing a flute, the others looking upwards in fear. Above them an angel, blessing them, on the other side the magi, on horseback and in regal robes point to the star. Above the grotto a multitude of angels in the clouds carrying a scroll with these words 'Glory to God in the highest and on earth be peace, goodwill towards man'. A great ray of light descends upon Christ's head.'

Didron, M., *Christian Iconography*, London 1886, vol. II, pp. 299–300

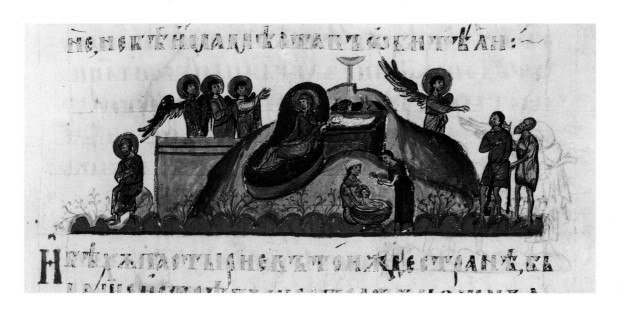

35 The Incarnation of Christ, incorporating the arrival of the Magi (f.142).

The key elements of this nativity scene in fact date back to the early Byzantine, pre-iconoclastic period and are a standard feature of cave and grotto art after the ninth century. This standard scene, one of two types which developed in Byzantine art, was then imbued with imperial iconography, so that the magi become paralleled with the Byzantine emperor.

The nativity scene is depicted twice – in Matthew and Luke – and both representations depart from the traditional composition, in different respects, as well as differing in style from one another. The miniature in the Gospel of St Matthew (fig. 37) is distinguished by its transformation of the arrival of the Magi into the Adoration, usually (though not always) depicted separately, and by further developing the story by adding the departure of the magi on their horses. (The liturgical role of the book may be of relevance here, as the arrival of the magi was celebrated on Christmas Day). The multitude of angels has been reduced, as has the number of shepherds and sheep outside the cave. These alterations were certainly not in the original scheme: traces of earlier outlines of the horses' feet remain on the left-hand side of the grotto where the arrival would have been depicted, and the white pigment used to cover the figures is still visible. Stylistic elements reveal that a different hand from the miniaturist's contributed to this change. The depiction of the three magi in the adoration and the departure reveals the spatial awareness and vibrance characteristic of the Renaissance master, while

the simpler, more remote presentation and gentler colours of the characters in the grotto, dominated by the serene stillness of the Virgin Mary, is more characteristic of the style of the archaic master.

The lively rendering of the horses, juxtaposed with the archaic style of the shepherds' features, emphasises the two different stylistic contributions in the production of this complex nativity image and reinforces the theme of the manifestation of god in man. The change reveals the impact of the Renaissance vision of the principal master, engaged in an artistic dilemma regarding what artistic devices to apply in order to achieve a more humanistic representation of the gospels' essential message. The remains of the horses' feet do indeed look grotesque within the intimate space of the nativity, while the more vigorous depiction of the three kings, kneeling in adoration and presenting their gifts of gold, frankincense and myrrh, to represent kingship, divinity and immortality, appears to be a more coherent continuation of the humble and beautiful Mary with her infant in the cradle.

The composition further continues its antithetical effect in the representation of the magi developed on a linear scale, while the towering composition of the grotto is emphasised with descending rays of light. These additions which one might expect to alter the composition in fact make it uniquely accomplished, as the completed design reveals a pure geometrical scheme governed by the ratio of the Vesica Piscis ('two fishes') (fig. 36) diagram. Every figure fits the diagram's proportions and follows the geometrical ratio with internal consistency. This diagram was considered as the domi-

36 The Nativity, showing the influence of the 'Vesica Piscis' diagram in its construction (f.10).

nant symbol of medieval Christian mysticism, representing the union of heaven and earth, 'above and below', creator and creation. The effect of this sophisticated cross-shaped composition, adding a sacred dimension to the illustration, seems to have been lost in the other Nativity miniature in the Gospel of St Luke (fig.35) which is probably the work of canonical disciple, as it follows the standard iconography of the nativity.

This remarkable change in the iconographic scheme also betrays an attempt to integrate the iconography of the gospels with contemporary hagiography within which the worship of the mother of god as protector and mediator was particularly strong. The local character of the features and clothing of the magi is appropriate to the devotion of the Bulgarian believer of the fourteenth century, differing greatly from the elongated features of the magi from the Paris Gospel. The iconographic innovation of the nativity scene from the Gospel

of St Matthew is certainly an outstanding monument to the Renaissance inspiration of the Turnovo School.

The theme of Jesus' genealogy, is treated in full in the Gospel of St Matthew, in five miniatures (*see* figs 1 and 4), and the same subject features again in the Gospel of St Luke in two miniatures (*see* fig.6), exemplifying the collaborative work of the scriptorium. The images in fig.1 suggest the contribution of the Academic master, while the vivid portrayal on f.7 (fig.4) and on f.147 (fig.6) is probably the work of the Renaissance master.

The miniatures related to the Baptism are of uniform quality, suggesting the further participation of the scriptorium. The rather rigid and dramatic appearance of John the Baptist in the scene depicting the Baptism of the people (fig.26), in contrast with the more amiable character portrayed on folio 13 (fig.28) in the baptism of Jesus on the River Jordan (personnified as an old man), is consistent with popular representations of the Baptist in Balkan iconography.

The Gospel of St John in particular provides additional illumination of the events associated with John the Baptist and his disciples. It also depicts events of moral

ТЪПРИНКЛАШЕВЬСЪНЪ,НЕВЪЗВРА
ТИШЖСАКЪНРОДОУ,ИИНЕМЛЪЖ
ТЕМЬОТИДОШЖВЪСТРАНЖ
СВОЖ:

ѠШЕДШЕМЛЖЕНИМЬ,СЕАГГЛЪГНЬ
ВЬСЪНЪIАВИСАIѠСИФОУГЛА·ВЪ

(*Above*)
37 The Nativity,
including the
adoration and
departure of the Magi
(f.10).

ЖЕГОЛАЖ·ИПРИКОСНЖСАРЖЦЪЕЖ·
ИѠСТАВИЖѠГНЬ·ИВЪСТАВЪИ
СЛОУЖААШЕИЕМОУ:

ВЕТЕРОУЖЕБЫВШОУ·ПРИВЕДОШХ

ОТЬ ЦИ ПЕТРОВЪ·

(*Left*)
38 Christ heals St
Peter's mother-in-
law (f.25).

(*Right*)
39 Cripples by the pool of Bethesda (above) and Jesus healing a man infirm for 38 years (f.225).

(*Below*)
40 Christ casts out evil spirits into swine (f.162v).

significance such as the expulsion of the money lenders from the Temple (fig.42), and the stoning of Christ by the Jews (fig.43).

The journey scenes – the flight into Egypt (fig.44), and the entry into Jerusalem (fig.59) are similar in composition and execution and abound in pastoral detail.

The events related to the subcycle of the miracles are represented with systematic regularity within each gospel. The exploration of an allegorical motif – the dramatic lighting in the miniatures of the Transfiguration from the Gospel of St Matthew (fig.45), which avoids the crude effect of light emanating from the mandorla of Christ, is in contrast with the simpler representations of the scene from the Gospel of St Mark and the Gospel of St Luke (fig.46), reminiscent of the popular style of presenting the light as intense and blazing. Christ's appearance to his disciples Peter, James and John on Mount Tabor was seen by the Hesychasts as the key event for the expression of their ideology of

НАВЕЧЕВ РОЖАЕ   ВПАТОСНАДЦАТОЕ

НСЪНИДЕСЪННИМАНПРНИДЕВЪНАЗАРЕТЪ ·
НЕ ̄БПОВННОУЖСАНИМА · НМ ̄ТНЕГОСЪБЛЮ

ИАКОНАПНСАНОЕСТЪ · ZАВНСТЬДО
МОУТВОЕГОСЪН ̄ЕСТЪНИА :

ОНZГНАНЫ ̄ ̈ЦРКВЕ

АZЪНШ ̄ЦЪ ЕДНН ̄ОЕС ̄ВЪ · ВЪ ZАШ ̄ЖЕ
КАМЕНÏЕПАКЫНОУД ̄ЕНДАПОБНЖ ̄ТЬЕГО :

(*Above, top*)
41 Mary and Joseph find the child in the temple (f.144v).

(*Above, centre*)
42 Christ expelling the money lenders from the Temple (f.217).

(*Left*)
43 Jews cast stones at Christ (f.243).

(*Above*)
44 The flight into Egypt (f.10v).

(*Right*)
45 The Transfiguration: Christ's miraculous appearance to his disciples Peter, John and James (f.51).

(*Below*)
46 The Transfiguration (f.166v).

(*Above, top*) 47 The miracle of the wedding at Cana (f.217).
(*Above*) 48 Apostles fishing with Christ; and the miracle at sea (f.150v).

'uncreated light', and the style thereafter flourished alongside more conservative representations sometimes seen in later church decoration in the schools of Tryavna and Arbanasee.

With their complex scenery and extensive group portrayals, the illuminations relating to the healing miracles are further complicated by curious small black creatures, usually depicted in packs. These devils and evil spirits, whose beginning as fallen angels is depicted in the miniature of the fall of Satan (fig.50), are shown in several miniatures being cast out by Jesus with a blessing gesture forgiving their sins, while a crowd looks on in astonishment (fig.40). Further miniatures which draw together references to more than one scene include the healing of Peter's mother-in-law (fig.38)

where the insertion of a banqueting scene, most probably derived from the Last Supper, imbues the miracle with the symbolism of the Eucharist. This is also a characteristic of the miniature of the miracle of the wine at the marriage feast of Cana, depicted in St John's Gospels, and of the miracles related to the sea (figs 47 and 48). The refined simplicity of the design is exquisitely enhanced by the use of azure and gold. The accompanying text refers to 'he whom even the sea and winds obey', while the miniatures represent Christ gracefully walking on water and calming the storm (fig.10). This extensive series of miniatures reflects an important liturgical principle in Byzantine gospel illumination, where water scenes are symbolically related to the Eucharist and the Baptism of Christ.

The representations of the feeding of the multitude bear the strongest impressionistic touches, as if the event has been captured on the spot, particularly distinguished by some neat group portraits (figs 10 and

НАБНЕОУ҆Е҆ДНОУ҆ЧЕННӸСВОХ҃ВЛѢСТН
ВЫКОРАБЛЬ НↃВАРНТНЕГОПАО҆НↃҐПОЛↃЫКↃ
ВНↃↃСА҆НДѢ · ДОↃↃДЕЖЕСА҆МЬⷬⷮↃПОУ҆СТНТↃ
НАРОДЫ · КО ҃ ӴЁ

НↃ҃ЮРЕКСА҆НↃ҃ДӒↃ҃ · НДЁВЬГОРↃХ҃ПӦМ̈ОЛНТНСӒ ·
НКЁӴЕОУ҆БЫВШОУ҃ · В̈ Т҃ КОРӒБЛЬ҃ПОↃ҃РѢ̈ДↃ̈

49 The miracle of the feeding of the multitude (f.104).

49). The distribution of bread and wine to the apostles (fig. 52) makes a contribution to the development of the frieze type of miniature, where Jesus seems to be merging behind the altar table while the apostles approach from either side. In the Paris Gospels (BN, MS grec 74) the two representations of Jesus show him by the sides of the table while in the sixth-century Rossano Gospel the event takes place in two successive scenes.

The climax of the miracles cycle – the resurrection of Lazarus (St John II 43–45, fig. 51) is represented in a powerful and dynamic frieze composition, conveying the narrative 'He said with a loud voice, Lazarus, come forth, and he that was dead came forth'.

50 Christ telling the disciples about the Fall of Satan (f.169v).

52 Christ distributing bread and wine to his disciples (f.202).

The Parables Cycle

The parables are the primary didactic element of the Gospels, and the second largest illuminated cycle in the Gospels of Tsar Ivan Alexander. The cycle's 107 miniatures represent the required 40 scenes in full, most lavishly in the Gospel of St Matthew, but with more individual miniatures in the Gospel of St Luke, as if to reinforce Luke's ambition to reveal the life of Jesus with the deepest understanding.

The cycle opens with the miniature on f.15 representing Christ teaching the beatitudes and the ten commandments. Along with the miniature on f.17 illuminating the teaching of the Lord's Prayer and the teaching of the eternal spiritual treasures, further illustrated with miniatures on 20, 21v and 23, followed by the illustra-

tion of the teaching of true justice, it forms the major short cycle of this section. The young Jesus is represented in traditional style, with reserve, suggesting the hand of the second master at work. The variation in the colouring of Jesus's garments (on f.15v, a gold toga over a blue robe, on f.17 a blue toga over a brown robe), accompanied by weaker portraiture, suggests further participation by the disciples in the scriptorium in these miniatures.

The most exquisite short cycle is that related to the disciples' initiation into the power of spiritual majesty, (fig. 5). The transitional style dominated by the studious portrayal of Christ with an exaggerated torso, is also suggestive of the hand of the second master.

The frieze-like composition is another Palaeologan return to the classics, used as a practical device for economy of space, as well as an ideal technical opportunity for grouping coherent miniatures into units,

uninterrupted by text. Here the massive two-fold compressed scenes surrounded by schematic architectural motifs, developing into a three-fold structure, is governed by a zigzag reading code, starting from the bottom, where Jesus is seen at a tender age, moving up to the top where he is shown white-haired, suggesting spiritual growth. The development of the structure under the influence of the meaning of the narrative occurred in other media too – the teaching of the principles of the faith, focusing on spiritual majesty, elaborated upon popular patristic teaching of the Theophylactus, Archbishop of Ochrid (*c.*1050–after

1126) became a canonical preface of many Slavonic gospels copied after the fourteenth century.

The main short parable cycle opens with the miniature of the unjust servant on f.53v in the gospel of St Matthew, followed by the miniatures on ff.53v (fig.53) and 54v, showing Christ teaching the necessity of assuming the innocence of a child in order to enter the kingdom of heaven. The illustrations of the parables of the seed and the sower (fig.57), the vineyard (fig.56), the lost sheep, the prodigal son, and of the seed which bore a tree as a home for birds (figs 23 and 24), reveal an impressive grasp of natural subjects such as birds,

(*Above*)
55 Christ teaching the instruments of Passion, showing the rich man in Hell (f.188).

(*Left*)
56 The parable of the vineyard where labourers worked for five pennies a day (f.59).

(*Below*)
57 The parable of the seed and the sower (f.96).

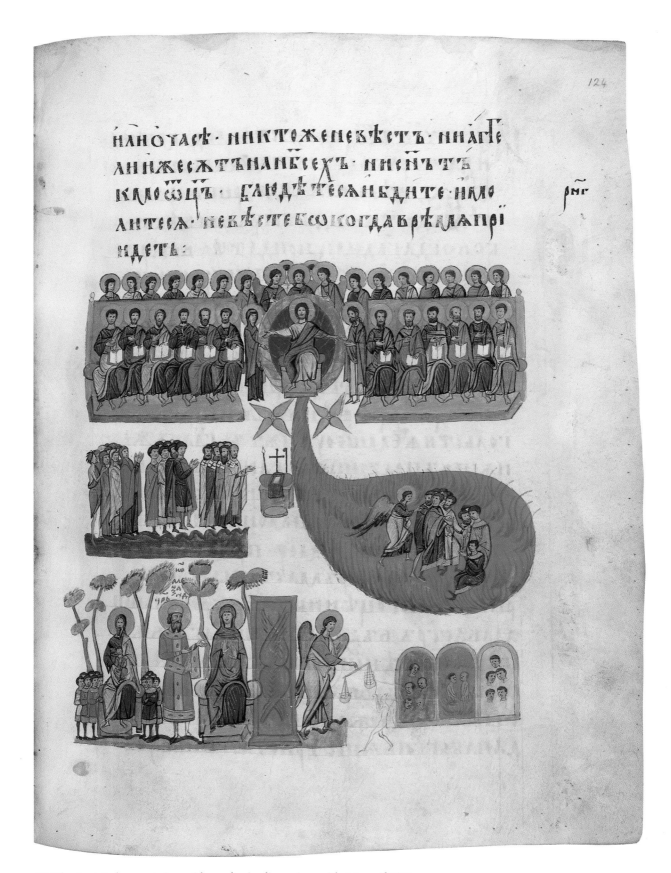

58 The Last Judgement; Ivan Alexender in discussion with Mary (f.124).

trees and vegetation complementing the symmetry and balance of the overall design. All are carefully observed, in the manner of the archaic master and bear witness to the Turnovo artists' interpretative skills, transmitting the divine word in an accessible and attractive way.

This attribute is further exemplified in the craftsmanship of the battle scene relating the prophecy of the destruction of the temple of Jerusalem at the beginning of the apocalyptic teaching of Mark and Luke (figs 7 and 8), strongly reminiscent of the many battle scenes in the contemporary Chronicle of Manasses, also produced in Turnovo. This is followed by the masterpiece of the cycle, the only example of a full-page miniature, that representing the Last Judgement (fig.58), from the Gospel of St Mark, which allows the last words of the teaching of Mark to serve as a guide to the final cycle of the Apocalypse. A similar miniature seems to have been removed from the Gospel of St Matthew since f.55, which in the Paris Gospel (BN, MS grec 54) contains the illumination of the last judgement, is missing, and the text is interrupted from Mark 25, 39–46.

The customary three-tier composition represents the three scales of judgement, consisting of the weighing of souls, the separation of the elect and the damned, and finally Jesus in Majesty, surrounded by the court of his holy mother on his right, John the Baptist on his left, and the twelve apostles seated with open books, while the back is occupied by saints, patriarchs and martyrs.

A few adaptations of the iconography which was established early in the post-iconoclastic era have been introduced: the palm branches which the saints would normally hold have been omitted; Jesus is seen in his usual brown clothes rather than in his white robe, and his blessing gesture has been modified to one with a more welcoming effect. On the first tier is Paradise with Abraham and the souls of the innocent, Mary on a throne at the gate of paradise, guarded by a four-winged cherubim. The abbot depicted in the Paris Gospel (BN, MS grec 74) has been replaced by the Tsar Ivan Alexander, who appears in his red royal garb in discussion with the virgin, as if praying for mercy for his subjects. This historical element creates a contemporary context for the terrifying weighing of souls proceeding alongside. On the second tier, on the right of Christ are the elect worshipping the judge's throne, while in fire on the left of Christ, are the sinners, cast out at his presence and condemned, along with the traitor Judas. The horror of the scene, known in Bulgarian as the 'terrible judgement' which for several centuries had been a corner-stone of Orthodox art, is reduced by depicting it on a symbolic level, motivated once again by the humanistic imperative of the time.

This scene incorporates two of the most popular iconic presentations in Orthodox art – Christ Pantocrator (Christ in majesty) and Deisis (Christ in majesty surrounded by John the Baptist and the Virgin); the Virgin was regarded in eastern legend as a mediator appearing at the day of judgement to plead for grace for sinners. A twelfth-century Bulgarian copy of an earlier apocryphal source 'The harrowing of the mother of God into hell' describes a dramatic journey of the Virgin into hell, guided by the Archangel Michael, reminiscent of the hell of Dante's *Divine Comedy*. The result is a cathartic prayer by the Virgin imploring the Lord's mercy and it is probable that post-iconoclastic iconography reflected this cult through the prominence of the Virgin's figure in the composition.

The present interpolation of the figure of the Tsar into the scene of the Last Judgement continues an earlier model of the relation of the Tsar and judgement, that of the first Bulgarian Christian monarch, Boris I in 864, and recorded by Theophanes Continuatus:

The Bulgarian ruler Boris, who was consumed by a great passion for hunting, wished to represent subjects of that kind in one of the houses that he used frequently, so that he might enjoy their sight by day and night. Seized by this desire, he summoned one of our Roman monks, a painter named Methodius, and when the latter came into his presence, he commanded him (through some divine inspiration) to paint not the killing of men in battle or the slaughter of wild beasts, but anything he might wish, on condition that the sight of the painting would induce fear and amazement in its spectators. The painter, who did not know of any subject more apt to inspire fear than the Second Coming of the Lord, depicted it there with the righteous on one side receiving the reward of their labour, and the sinners on the other, reaping the fruits of their misdeeds and being harshly driven away to the punishment that had been threatened to them. When he (Boris) had seen the finished painting, he conceived thereby the fear of God and after being instructed in the Holy mysteries, he partook of divine Baptism in the dead of night.

Mango, C., *The Art of the Byzantine Empire 312–1453*, Toronto, 1986, pp.190–1

Five centuries later, the Tsar is shown as intrinsic to the sublime Christian act, developed now as a symbol of the monarch's ultimate authority as protector and leader of his people.

ДЕВАКН·ТАИПАСЪОБ·ВЛА'НАДЕСАТЕ:

Н·ВЬОҮТРѢНІЙ·НZШЕДШЕМЬНМЪ·Ѿ·ВН

СИЛАѠНЬПЕТРЪ·ГЙ·НЕНОZѢ́ЛМОНТЪ
КЛЛО·МЖ҄НРЖ҄ЦѢ́НГЛАВЖ:

ЛАIЕМОҮ IС·НZЛЛЬВЕНЫНПЕТРЪ·КОҮIЕТЬ

(*Above, top*) 59 Christ's entry into Jerusalem (f.117).

(*Above*) 60 The Holy Ablution (f.251).

The Passion Cycle

The climax of the life of Christ has been formalised as a precise narrative in traditional iconography. The text of three chapters only was to be illuminated, in 35 miniatures, providing a dense series of pictorial representations. The artists of the Gospels of Tsar Ivan Alexander have dedicated 102 miniatures to the Passion, of which the Gospel of St John offers a complete account, with 36 miniatures, its largest cycle, concentrating on the highest theological subject matter. The opening scene of the cycle, the Holy Ablution (fig.60) is remarkable for the quality of its detail of movement and gesture, and at the same time is deeply spiritual. The simple portrayal of Jesus without a mantle and with turned up sleeves is full of immediacy, while the bare-footed disciples have assumed a variety of postures of embarrassment and astonishment. The scene was widely favoured in Orthodox teaching of humility, revealed in Jesus' response to Peter's protest: 'If I do not wash you, you can have no part with me.' (John 13:8)

The miniature of the last supper follows the Balkan style, with an oval table with either a blue or red marble finish (figs 61 and 65). The composition has been subsequently altered, with Jesus sitting on the left side

СЛѢРАВВЙ; ГЛАІЕЛЛОУТЫРЕТЕ:

ДХШЕЛЛЖЕНХЛХ, ПРИЕЛЛХЇС ХЛѢБХ, Н

61 The Last Supper
(f.76v).

БЫТН:

ВХТХ ЧАРЕЧЕЇС НАРОДОКЛЬ · ІАКОНАРАЗБО
ННИКАЛНИЗХІЛОСТЕ СХШОХЖЖННН

62 Christ's betrayal
and arrest (f.78v).

(*Below*)
63 Christ and disciples
enter the garden of
Gethsemene (f.126v).

ЛЛХІЕГДАВХСКРХСПХ, ВАРХВЫКХГАЛІЛЕН:~

ПЕТРХЖЕРЕЕ́ЕЛЛОУ · АШЕИВСЕ́СХБЛАЗНА
ТСА, НЖНЕАЗХ · НГЛАЕЛЛОУЇС · АЛЛННХ

ПОЗД҃Ѣ ЖЕ КЫ В Ш ОУ, ПРИИДЕ Ч҃ К Ъ КОГАТ҃
Ѡ҃ АРИМА·Ѳ҃ЕА · ИЛЕНЕМЛЫ ІѠСИФЪ · ИЖЕ
НТ҃ ОУЧИЛЬСА К҃ОУ ІС҃А · СЪ ПРИСТ҃ЖПИ
КЫ ПИЛАТОУ, ПРОСИТ҃ Ѣ ЛА ІС҃ВА · ТОГДА
ПИЛАТЪ ПОВЕЛ҃Ѣ ДАТИ Т҃ѢЛО ІС҃ВО · И ПРИ
ЕМЪ Т҃ѢЛО ІѠСИФЪ · ОБВИТЬ Е ПЛАЩА
НИЦЕѦ ЧИСТОѦ · И ПОЛОЖИ ВЪ НОВ҃ѢМЬ
СВОЕМЪ ГРОБ҃Ѣ · ИЖЕ И С҃ѢЧЕ ВЪ КАМЕНИ

64 The Crucifixion (f.84).

(Above) 65 The Last Supper (St Luke's Gospel) (f.202v).

(Left) 66 Christ awakes his sleeping disciples (f.127).

(Below) 67 Christ arrested and brought before Pilate (f.80).

(Opposite, above) 68 Christ tormented on the cross (f.208v).

(Opposite, below) 69 The descent from the cross and the entombment of Christ (f.84v).

rather than occupying a central place. The perspective, from ground level, creates an intriguing effect: the table looks monumental, while Jesus and the apostles seem remote, as if the artist or spectator was prostrated on the ground in awe and wonder at the scene.

The depiction of the betrayal scenes reveals in many small details the pathos of the narrative. Judas's halo has been removed in the conspiracy scene on f.75. Judas's betraying kiss is presented in traditional fashion, central to a group picture (fig.62), while the final scene related to the prophesy – that of Judas hanging himself – is shown only in St Matthew's Gospel (f.80v).

The composition of the miniatures in the central cycle – the agony, arrest, appearance before Pilate, crucifixion, lamentation, resurrection and ascension, continues the canonical scheme, while their representation takes a more dramatic form. The scene of the agony (fig.66) offers an interesting design variation, blending into the text as a floating miniature. The trauma of the apostle Peter is portrayed in some detail – he is seen weeping on ff. 80, 205, and 262.

The crucifixion scenes are of varied quality. The sequence in Matthew, representing Christ in three successive scenes, is perhaps designed to influence the presentation of the narrative in other media, presumably the lectionary readings for Good Friday. The great crucifixion scene is in the traditional iconographical style, with Christ nailed on the cross between the two thieves in the distance, immediately above the crowd, with the centurions and open graves on the ground (fig.64). The graphic monumentality of the scene has been controlled with refined and quiet colouring and Jesus has assumed an idealised appearance, balanced by the prominent curve of his figure, in the Balkan style. The artist has succeeded in reviving it and giving it a new artistic dimension. The disregard for the naturalistic details of Christ's wounds, often represented in western art, compliments the wholesome spirit of the depiction, motivated by the Orthodox idea of transcending earthly sorrow and focusing on the resurrection and ascension. The figure of Mary is particularly moving, as she touches her face with Christ's hand, while Joseph of Arimathea stands on the right-hand side of Christ lost in sorrow. The crucifixion scene on f.132 is more schematic, while the one on f.208v (fig.35) is interesting for its representation of a realistic-looking green, rough cross.

The approach to the two representations of the descent into hell differs quite markedly: one (fig.18) is in the Byzantine tradition while that on f.85 (fig.17) portrays Christ in unassailable majesty, reminiscent of the famous Macedonian Renaissance Hercules type of the resurrected Christ. This image of the saviour, who frees Adam and Eve, probably developed under the liturgical influence of the feast of the twelve apostles.

The Ascension (figs 32 and 33), a favourite scene in the Balkan tradition, designed to epitomise the elevation of the spirit and its fulfilment through salvation, shows the main figures hierarchically, with Jesus in the mandorla in the left margin and Mary, Magdalina and the Apostles following in turn on the ground. This contrasts markedly with their arrangement as a central group in the late twelfth-century Byzantine gospel-book, British Library Harley MS 1810.

Following the narrative, the Gospel of St John offers additional scenes after the Ascension such as the touch of the doubting Thomas and the appearance of Christ to Mary at the tomb (fig.19) and to his disciples on the Lake of Tiberius (ff.270, 271v). The Gospels provide clear evidence that the readings from the Passion were treated as a separate unit, and the manuscript bears witness to the existence of an elaborate liturgical system which was undoubtedly a challenge for the artist, who had to model his pictorial representations upon it.

Conclusion: Some Comparisons

The Gospels of Tsar Ivan Alexander occupies a prominent place in the evolution of the iconography of extensive gospel illumination. Of illustrated gospel-books which have come down to us, the earliest, the Rossano Gospel (sixth century) represents the Alexandrian recension, while the Antiochan recension is retained in the two post-iconoclastic examples, the eleventh-century Byzantine gospel in Florence (Biblioteca Medicia Laurenziana, Laur. Plut. 23) and in the other late eleventh-century Byzantine Gospel mentioned earlier (Paris, MS Grec 74), created in the Studion Monastery of Constantinople. The Gospels of Tsar Ivan Alexander is even more closely related to its fourteenth-century Bulgarian religious and cultural context, and represents the establishment of a revised aesthetic idiom.

The Gospels displays the same Antiochan recension as the early eleventh-century Paris Gospels, but certain iconographic differences reveal that it is derived from different prototypes. The Gospels of Tsar Ivan Alexander is in a larger format and contains four extra miniatures, including the important ascension scene in St Luke's Gospel (fig.33), the presentation miniature and most importantly the royal portrait over a double spread (fig.11). The Paris Gospels offers eight other miniatures and its style is characteristic of the first post-iconoclastic Comnenian revival, with its hieratic style and idealised mannerism. The Gospels of Tsar Ivan Alexander represents the evolution of the concept of ecclesiastic and imperial synthesis, strongly expressed in the rich royal cycle of six miniatures which required several compositional changes and additions (one of the most notable being the substitution of the abbot in the presentation scene of the Paris gospels with the Tsar). Some fourteenth-century liturgical developments relating to the characteristically Balkan practice, particularly strong in Bulgaria, of worship of the Mother of God, determined further changes in the treatment of the Nativity cycle (fig.37), initiating the theme of the Adoration of the Magi rather than the Arrival of the Magi.

The style of the Gospels of Tsar Ivan Alexander reveals an interesting exploration of the major Byzantine vocabulary of the archaic and academic, specifically of the Turnovo recension which embodied a Renaissance humanist inspiration, effectively transforming the more illustrative 'art mignon' into a more explicit art. The development of the frieze miniature reflects the further trend towards the abandonment of

70 Jesus Christ, Tsar Ivan Alexander and the chronicler Manasses, from the fourteenth-century Bulgarian manuscript (Vatican Library, MS Slav. 2, f.1v).

borders and towards bringing related scenes together into compressed frieze cycles (seen in several miniatures) (ff. 239 and 267v). In all the Gospels comprises 630 individual scenes, compressed into 367 miniatures. For example, in fig. 54 the parable of the ten virgins is shown as one scene, whereas it appears as two miniatures in the Paris Gospels and others. This tendency in promoting and elaborating upon the frieze miniature, along with the use of classical elements in the creation of the 'magic square' (*see* pages 26–27), and in the elaborate geometric composition of the royal portrait and the nativity (figs 29 and 36) are unique characteristics of the Turnovo school's high academic profile and unique contributions to this style. It is thus likely that the Gospels of Tsar Ivan Alexander had a more archaic prototype, which when adapted by the highly creative aesthetic idiom of the Turnovo school, produced the climax of the style's development.

It is not surprising therefore that the Gospels had a seminal effect on the further evolution of the extensive scheme of illuminations. The first example of this is the Gospels' conventional counterpart, now known as the Elisavetgrad Gospels, in the church of Pocrofvsky Sobor, also produced in Turnovo before the end of the fourteenth-century. It is in Bulgarian, in the same format, and contains 355 miniatures, but the style is less ambitious, and since the royal cycle has been omitted it is likely that it was not produced in the same scriptorium, which was particularly associated with the court art of Ivan Alexander, and from which there are two other surviving examples. However, it does indicate the immediate influence that Ivan Alexander's masterpiece had on Bulgarian art.

The other two surviving contemporary manuscripts from the royal library of Ivan Alexander – the Tomic Psalter, with 58 miniatures (Moscow CIM, MS Syn. 2752), famous for its elaborate illustration of the Akathistos hymn, and the secular Chronicle of Manasses, with 69 miniatures (Vatican Library, MS Slav. 2, fig. 70), bear witness to the diverse artistic endeavour of the Turnovo school and together could be imagined to form sort of trinity arising from it.

Further recensions of the Gospels of Tsar Ivan Alexander are seen in the Wallachian Gospels of Suchava Monastery in Romania (Suchevitsa MS 23), from the sixteenth-century, and the Moldavian gospel-book (Suchevitsa MS 24), from the seventeenth-century, both written in Bulgarian. Suchevitsa 23 is the most likely direct descendant of the Gospels of Ivan Alexander, as it follows the same ecclesiastical/imperial concept, according to which the portraits of the Wallachian rulers – Voivod Ivan Alexander (1568–1577) and his son Voivod Ivan Michnea have been incorporated at the end of the gospels. The archaic style has been favoured, but the innovation of the Nativity combined with the Adoration of the Magi is also reflected in some of the details; since at that time the Gospels of Tsar Ivan Alexander was in the library of the Wallachian court, having been purchased by the Wallachian Ivan Alexander, it seems likely that the second gospel-book was directly copied from the first.

Suchevitsa 24, with its 355 miniatures, is the most eclectic example from this group, with a conventional approach and an iconographic system which suggests that one of its sources was probably Suchevitsa 23 or the Elisavetgrad Gospels. The omission of the royal cycle and the stereotyped rendering, with a preference for an over-rich decorative scheme, might be explained by the further remoteness of the copy from its unprovincial academic prototype, and the fact that it appears to have been influenced by popular contemporary patterns. The note by the Romanian Mount Athos monk, Gabriel, on one of the last pages of the Gospels of Ivan Alexander, saying that he copied the book indicates that the book became a prototype for the Mount Athos scriptoria.

The Gospels of Tsar Ivan Alexander can thus be seen as the climax of the evolution of an extensive Byzantine scheme of illumination, introducing several important innovations. The Royal portrait, with its Renaissance style, classicised composition and conceptual significance, the Nativity with its important compositional innovation, the explicit exploration of a more illustrative style, and the invention of the palindrome of Ivan Alexander, all contribute to its highly original character and historical value.

AN OUTLINE OF THE STRUCTURE AND CONTENTS OF THE GOSPELS OF TSAR IVAN ALEXANDER

British Library Additional MS 39627

The manuscript has a magnificent appearance, in its original stamped crimson leather binding, decorated with a geometrical pattern and the image of a gryphon (fig.71). The leather is on wooden boards, probably reused. There is a spine of 8cm, slightly raised in the standard Byzantine manner. Symmetrically arranged holes indicate where precious stones originally decorated the cover. Some large holes, containing the remains of rusty nails, suggest that there was once a protective cover, probably of gilt silver. The vellum is of good quality, occasionally affected by damp and subsequently repaired. The manuscript has 286 leaves and measures 240× 335mm, bound in standard gatherings of eight leaves. The last gathering (ff.276–84) is of smaller format, and is a later insertion.

CONTENTS

1   Table of miniatures compared with those of Paris, BN, MS Grec 74, by H. Ommont

1–2   Blank

2v–3   Royal portrait

THE GOSPEL OF ST MATTHEW

3v–4   Table of contents of the Gospels of St Matthew

4v   Blank

5   Note of the Moldavian Voivod Ivan Alexander

5v   Blank

6   Headpiece of the Gospel of St Matthew

6–86   The Gospel of St Matthew, including 104 miniatures

86v   St Matthew presenting his Gospel to Tsar Ivan Alexander

THE GOSPEL OF ST MARK

87   Table of contents of the Gospel of St Mark

87v   Blank

88   The headpiece of the Gospel of St Mark

88–134v   The Gospel of St Mark, including 65 miniatures.

88v   St Mark presents his Gospel

THE GOSPEL OF ST LUKE

135–136   Table of contents of the Gospel of St Luke

136v   Blank

137   The headpiece of the Gospel of St Luke

137–212   The Gospel of St Luke, including 100 miniatures

212v   St Luke presents his Gospel

THE GOSPEL OF ST JOHN

212v   Table of contents of the Gospel of St John

213   The headpiece of the Gospel of St John

213–272v   The Gospel of St John, including 90 miniatures

272v   St John presents his Gospel

f.273   Blank

THE ENDING

273v   The 'magic square'

274–275   The colophon of the scribe Simeon

275v   Blank; the bottom is signed 'LE' (not original)

ADDITIONS

The Gospels has separate lectionary marks including systematic notes in the margins of the folios indicating the sermon lessons

276–278   Menology, the calendar of the grand orthodox feast days and their readings, beginning on 1 September, the start of the orthodox church year

278–279   Guide to how and when to begin the study of the scriptures

279v   Blank

280–283v   Synaxaria (a calendar), with a list of readings for each feast day

The calligraphic character of the additional semi-uncial writings is varied. Some bear similarities with the more careful writing of the Menology, while others are consistent with the smaller and sharper writing of the Synaxaria

ADDITIONS UNRELATED TO THE TEXT

284–285v   Blank

286   Note in Romanian (in Cyrillic script): 'I, Hierodeacon Gabriel, have copied this when I was in the monastery of St Paul, to send it to the Romanian kingdom, and whoever [reads] to say "God have mercy on him" Signed Hierodeacon Gabriel'

286v   Note in Greek: 'The present Gospel of St Paul's a thousand and twenty'

Further Reading

The Gospels

The standard introduction to the Gospels of Tsar Ivan Alexander, with description, historical background, comparative notes, and a full set of illustrations in black and white, is the bilingual monograph (Bulgarian and French) by B. Filoff, *Miniaturite na Londonskoto Evangelie na Tsar Ivan Alexander/Les Miniatures de l'evangile du roi Jean Alexandre a Londres,* Sofia, 1934. Other reference works with accounts of the manuscript in Bulgarian are given below. A brief discussion of the manuscript is given in R. Curzon, *Catalogue of Materials for Writing,* London, 1849, pp.32–33 and in the most recent major compilation, R. Cleminson, *A Union Catalogue of Cyrillic Manuscripts in British and Irish Collections,* University of London, 1988, pp.121–123. A brief discussion of the Gospels' portraiture is provided by Ioanis Spatharakis in *The Portrait in Byzantine Illuminated Manuscripts,* Leiden, 1976, pp.67–70. Further discussion of comparative sources for the Gospels is provided by S. de Nersscssian in 'Two Slavonic Parallels for the Greek Tetraevangelia, Paris 74', in the *Art Bulletin,* vol.IX, n.3, pp.223–274.

Bulgarian and Byzantine Art

A comprehensive study of Bulgarian medieval art, with black-and-white illustrations, is A. Grabar, *La peinture religieuse en Bulgarie,* 1928; Renaissance elements in Bulgarian medieval art are further discussed by D. Talbot-Rice in his *Art of the Byzantine Era,* Thames and Hudson, 1993, pp.190–194. A standard work on Byzantine art is A. Grabar, *Art of the World, Byzantium,* Holland, 1966; *see also* K. Weitzman, *Illustrations in roll and codex: a study of the origin and method of text illumination,* Princeton University Press, 1970; P. A. Michaelis, *An aesthetic approach to Byzantine Art,* London, 1964; and E. Panofsky, *Studies in Iconology,* New York, 1939. On the Renaissance in Byzantine art, a comparative discussion is provided by E. Panofsky in *Renaissance and Renaissances in Western Art,* Stockholm, 1960, and the Renaissance style of Manuel Pancelinos is discussed by P. Underwood in *Archaeology,* New York, vol.X, n.3, pp.215–216. For techniques and methods

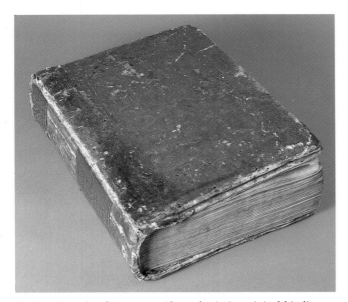

71 The Gospels of Tsar Ivan Alexander in its original binding.

of Byzantine iconography (after Pancelinos), *see* the details provided from the 'Hermeneya of Dionysios of Phorna' incorporated in the first-hand source, M. Didron, *Manuel d'Iconographie Chretienne Greque et Latine . . . traduit du manuscrit Byzantine, Le Guide de la Peinture par Paul Durand,* Paris, 1845. The most recent practical guide is G. Ramos-Poqui, *The Technique of Icon Painting,* Burns and Oates/Surch Press, 1990, which also provides a brief insight into the 'sacred' geometry, pp.60–66. More detail on the same is given by Robert Lawlor, *Sacred Geometry – philosophy and practice,* Thames and Hudson, 1990. Other interesting accounts of first-hand sources for Byzantine art are C. Mango, *The Art of the Byzantine Empire 312–1453,* Toronto, 1973, and the catalogue of an exhibition in honour of K. Waitzman, *Illuminated Greek Manuscripts from the American Collections,* Princeton University Press, 1986.

Spiritual Background

A comprehensive account of the spiritual background to iconography is given by A. Remisov in *The Spiritual Meadow,* St Paul's book and media centre, 1989 and in L. Genaudius in *Icons – Windows of Eternity,* Geneva, 1990, as well as in M. Quenot, *The Icon – Window of the Kingdom,* Crestwood, 1991. For further reading on iconoclasm, *see* R. Cormack, *Writing in Gold,* London, 1985, pp.91–141.

The Scripts

On Glagolitic and Cyrillic scripts, *see Cambridge Medieval History,* 1967, vol.II, p.510; A. Gaur, *A History of Writing,* The British Library, 1984, rev. ed. 1992, p.125; and R. Browning, *Byzantium and Bulgaria,* London, 1975, pp.144–145. Background to the art of the 'carmina figurata' used in the 'magic square' is included in D. Higgins, *Pattern Poetry,* State University Press of New York, Charles Doria, 'Visual Writing Forms in Antiquity', published in *West Coast Poetry Reading,* 19, Nevada, 1979, and Carl Nordenfalk, *Early Medieval Book Illumination,* Scira, 1988, pp.9–10.

Historical Background

For the historical background, *see* Steven Runsiman, *History of the First Bulgarian Empire,* London, 1930, R. Browning, *Byzantium and Bulgaria,* London, 1975; E. Gibbon, *The Decline and Fall of the Roman Empire,* 1845; N. Byrnes, *The Byzantine Empire,* Oxford University Press; A. Toynbee, *A Study of History,* London, 1972. A general account of the history of the Gospels itself is provided by Robert Curzon, *Visits to the Monasteries in the Levant,* London, 1916, pp.396–398. A. Achioritis, *Holy Mountain,* Thessalonica, 1970 also provides an interesting account of the treasures, history and life of the monastic communities of Mount Athos.

Works published in Bulgarian and Russian

A general description of the manuscript is also provided in P. Gudev, *Bulgarski rukopisy v bibliotgecata na Lord Zouche in Sbornik za Narodny Umotvorenia, Nauka i Knijnina,* 1892, vol.VII, pp.159–223 and vol.VIII, pp.137–168. An account of the Gospels is given by P. Syrku in *Sbornik Otdeleniya Ruskogo yazica i Slovesnosty, Academia nauk, LXXXIV, N"–XV,* pp.1–21, and F. Uspensky in *Zurnal Ministerstva Narodnogo Prosveshteniya,* 1878, vol.IX, part II, pp.9–21. Works on the historical background include D. Suselov, *Patya na Bulgarite,* Sofia, 1936; I. Andreev, *Bulgarskite Hanove i Tsare 7–14 vek,* Sofia, 1992; V. Zlatarski, *Istoria na Bulgarskata Darjava pres Srednite Vekove,* Sofia, 1970; I. Duichev, *Pateki na Utroto,* Sofia, 1985; and P. Dinekov, *Hristomatya po Starobulgarska Literatura,* Sofia, 1967.